CW01501866

PRAISE FOR *LOVE YOU BAD*

'A psychological thriller not to be missed'
Jessica Knott

'My heart was in my mouth'
Leanne Braithwaite

'I did not see *that* twist coming'
Heather Dubay

'Unputdownable'
Lisa Jenkins

'Very cleverly written'
Liz Hearne

'Claustrophobic'
J. C. Malone

'Spinetingling'
Caz Bower

'Twisted'
A. J. Thomas

'This book is the stuff nightmares are made of'
Jamie Curtis

'Filled with shocking revelations . . . kept me glued to my seat from the first page to the last'
Claire Bergh

'Just when you think you know where you're being led another shocking revelation slams into you, knocking everything you thought you knew back on its head . . . *Love You Bad* is an impressive take on the domestic noir genre . . . chilling, from the start to the nail-biting conclusion'
Lorna Okobo

'Atmospheric, unsettling, emotional . . . I cannot wait to read the sequel'
Joe Singleton

'A fast-paced read that will have you hooked from the first page'
Julie Lacey

'A thrilling read'
Chantelle Hazelden

'A compelling story that kept me on the edge of my seat'
Alyson Read

'A tense read [that] keeps you on a knife-edge'
Beyond The Books

'A real page-turner'
Linda Strong

'Gripping'
Wendy Robey

'Filled with danger and suspense'
Splashes Into Books

'Instantly intriguing . . . It's short and snappy with non-stop drama and action'
Two Ladies and a Book

'Creepy'
Brewtiful Fiction

'Unsettling'
Library of Lucy

'An intriguing read . . . impossible to put down . . . will leave your head spinning'
FeatzReviews

'A dark and brutal story'
Dawn's Book Reviews

'*Love You Bad* has a Pulp Fiction-esque narrative'
Read The Week

'I read this in a day . . . I couldn't get through it fast enough'
Honest M Reader

'A thrilling read that will grip you from the start and have you racing to the end in one sitting . . . A rollercoaster of a read'
Reading in the Light

'I am still thinking about this book days after I read it . . . I found each character extremely convincing and I went through a range of emotions as the story progressed'
Joy Wood

'A dark and disturbing tale . . . atmospheric writing and believable characters . . . you can't believe what you're reading, but you can't stop either'
Books in my Opinion

'Throughout this story there is a dark and dangerous undertone . . . I could feel the mounting tension'
Run Away Irish Girl

'A whirlwind suspense . . . an exciting, entertaining read that will keep you questioning what is real'
Cover2Cover

DARK EDGE PRESS

LOVE YOU BAD

LOUISE MULLINS

Published in 2021 by Dark Edge Press.

Y Bwthyn
Caerleon road,
Newport,
Wales.

www.darkedgepress.co.uk

Text copyright © 2021 Louise Mullins

Cover Design: Jamie Curtis

Cover Photography: Sertravelalot/Shutterstock

The moral right of Louise Mullins to be identified as the author of this work has been asserted in accordance with the Copyright, Designs and Patents Act 1988.

All rights reserved, including the right to reproduce this book, or portions thereof in any form. No part of this text may be reproduced, transmitted, downloaded, decompiled, reverse engineered, stored, or introduced into any information storage and retrieval system by any means, whether electronic or mechanical without the express written permission of the author.

This is a work of fiction. Names, characters, places, incidents and dialogues are products of the author's imagination or are used fictitiously. Any resemblance to actual people, living or dead, events or locales is entirely coincidental.

A catalogue record of this book is available from the British Library.

ISBN (eBook): B08BGT3C4L
ISBN (Hardback): 979-8-5129-9022-3

Ever Fallen in Love with (Someone You Shouldn't've)?
The Buzzcocks

In memory of Carrie and George. I wish you could have stayed around long enough to read this.

PROLOGUE

I stare down at the body at my feet, the blood on my hands. It's going to take me hours to clean up the mess, and I can't even begin to wipe away the evidence of my crime until I've found someplace to put the corpse. Somewhere no one will think to find it.

PART ONE

DOMINIC

Then

It wasn't love at first sight. I didn't notice her until she dropped a quarter from her palmful, collected from the slot machine flashing WIN!

I was hungry, tired, and wanted to drink myself into oblivion, so I'd taken my last ten cents and headed into the casino. I lost it on a game of roulette within minutes of entering. I had nowhere to go, my wallet was empty. Then she dropped that quarter.

I collected it from the red carpet, noted the gold rings on her fingers as I handed it to her. She smiled, turned away. I stood back and examined her. She was slimmer than her friend, though still pudgier than I was used to. Older too. But she wore her age with class. And she threw money in that machine like it didn't dent her purse. That's when I knew I had to go home with her. If I let her slip away I'd be spending the night in the subway with the junkies and I didn't want to wake up shoeless the next morning. Those bastards will nick anything worth a dollar.

Her friend tried to persuade her to stay. 'Have another drink,' she said. The universal language of women who felt uncomfortable in the presence of a man. What she meant was, 'Don't take him back to your room. You don't know him. What if he's a killer?'

She told her friend not to worry, promised to text her some secret code that would assure her she was safe and well later, and said – looking me in the eye – to call the cops if she didn't, and to knock on the door of her hotel suite to check that she was still alive first thing in the morning if she did. I had to bite the inside of my cheek to stop myself from blurting out how stupid I thought it was for her to give me such a long stretch of opportunity to choke, stab, or shoot her so-called bestie.

I let her take the lead, let her think she was in control as she led me from the casino and back to her suite. She closed the door behind us and walked me to the bed. The duvet was made from unruffled, high thread-count Egyptian cotton. The sheets were unstained. It was her first night in the hotel.

I chose this side of Las Vegas as it was just a quick walk from the casino that offered its compatriots free booze while they lost their money. That way I only had to stagger a couple of blocks to where my mate had been putting me up in his apartment.

I'd met him in the green room of a party where the drugs were delivered on silver trays like hors d'oeuvres by barely clothed waitresses. He liked my drifter lifestyle, said it was refreshing to meet a true bohemian and not a stoned, privately educated, trust funded student pretending to be one. With a woman on each arm he invited me and one other man back to his apartment. A woman laced her arms round the man's waist and another round mine. I stood and followed them out the door.

I don't remember much about that night, but I woke up with a sore dick and my fingernails were clotted with pussy juice and cocaine. I don't know what the guy did for a living, but he had tonnes of money and enjoyed wasting it, and I wasn't averse to helping him.

The only ones who survive Las Vegas have money or marry someone who does.

So back to the hotel room with the older woman whose midline rose over her hips and whose stretchmarks turned silver when the lamplight caught her thighs, bent over the bed with her skirt hitched up to her waist and her panties pulled aside to reveal the mound of hair between her legs. I closed my eyes and slammed into her, imagining she was younger, tighter. And when she pushed me in the stomach to stand I fought the urge to shove her face-down and fuck her until she cried my name. The internal war raged on until I pulled out of her.

She was vanilla in every sense of the word. Conservative. Respectable. And I knew that if I tried to change that she'd throw me out. So I clenched my jaw and let her tell me how to please her.

She turned round and smiled, sat on the edge of the bed, lay down, opened her legs, and tugged on the neckline of my shirt so that I fell on top of her. One part of her labia hung lower than the other and her tits swung like doorknockers as I pumped into her, which I did with an element of resistance I didn't know I possessed. Keeping a steady rhythm until the thick folds of her flesh grew slick and she came with a shudder.

I prised her red-painted talons from my shoulders and was glad when she headed straight for the bathroom to clean herself afterwards, uninterested in post-coital hugs. Which suited me fine as I could remove the small pair of panties from my trouser pocket, wrap them round my cock, close my eyes, and wank myself off to thoughts of the girl with the firm ass who writhed below me in my dreams.

She returned as I came with a grunt. I stuffed the

panties into the waste paper basket and knocked an empty packet of noodles on top of them. She didn't speak when she caught my eye, just threw the black lace-edged camisole over her head, the thin silk straps catching on her damp knotted hair, and lay back on the bed, out of breath, with a smile.

Pretending I hadn't already seen it, I pointed to her ring and said, 'You're a Mum.'

'I've got a daughter,' she said, lowering her gaze.

'How old?'

'Six.'

'Cool.'

'Some men, it puts them off having a relationship. That's why I've had no luck dating. They don't want the bother of taking on someone else's kid.'

'They're idiots.'

She grinned. 'Yeah, they are.'

'What's she like?' I lay on my side, facing her, resting my head on my fist.

'She's a good girl. Cute too. Her papa said she'll be a heartbreaker.'

'Is he around?'

'No. He died. He was a soldier. Got blasted by a landmine in Afghanistan.'

'I'm sorry.'

'He was good to me.'

'I'm glad.'

'You're not like the others.'

'The others?'

'There haven't been many lovers,' she said, resting a hand on the tense arm I used to hold my head up.

I trailed the backs of my fingers up her leg as she lay languid.

She sighed. 'You listen like you care. And you know what to do with a woman.' She placed her hand on mine and brought it up to her wet pussy.

I'd seen the MUM ring on her index finger as I passed her the quarter she'd dropped in the casino. The diamond solitaire on her middle finger, the rubies and sapphires bonded onto the chunky gold bands that climbed midway to her knuckles. She smelled of money and desperation. The perfect combination for a hustle.

KERENSA

Now

I twist the wedding band round my ring finger as I gaze at the vast expanse of land surrounding the back of our home. Dominic said I'd grow into it but it's still too big.

My face is pressed up against the window so I can smell the peppermint toothpaste on my breath. I rub the condensation away with the sleeve of my jumper, leaving a smear on the glass.

I lean back and rest my spine on the cushions of my window seat, reflecting on the face that stares at me. Her hollow-eyes, pale skin, dark hair, dry lips. She doesn't look how I feel. Content. Appreciative. Privileged. Instead she appears haunted.

Most would think me lucky, but every marriage has its secrets. Some people are just better at hiding them.

Beneath a cornflower blue sky lies the garden border, containing rows of shrubs and flowers. The stone yard in front of it, dotted by cherry blossom trees. Beyond that, the lush green field that ends at the entrance to the forest where the ferns frame the grounds. To the right, just out of my line of view, behind the hedge is the summerhouse where our wedding took place. The photographs destroyed in the flood, caused by the burst riverbank that runs alongside it, after the storm. Though Miss Bergh, Annika, our most recent au pair, told me the water couldn't possibly reach as far as our cliff-top mansion. Her face pinched with a scowl when I tried to put her right.

And she would know. I've never left the house.

'You must be mistaken,' she said. 'I've lived here since I arrived from Poland, in the nineties. The river has not burst its bank in all my thirty years. Besides, even if it had, this house is two levels above the floodplain which is sloped towards the sea.'

Did Dominic overhear?

Is that why my husband dismissed her?

I stand, take my empty beaker into the kitchen and head upstairs to the toilet. I don't make it as far as the bathroom before something lands on my nose. Wet like a raindrop. I look up at the ceiling and see a damp patch, slightly bowed, the white paint now urine yellow.

Dominic doesn't know the first thing about DIY. Won't ask for my advice despite the fact I've read every book shelved in the downstairs library, including those about household maintenance, and won't call a tiler – which is whom we likely need – because it'll mean letting a stranger into *his* home.

I enter the bathroom to pee, ignoring the cracked plasterboard, the wallpaper beneath it that's saturated and hangs above my head as I descend the stairs, pretending I can't hear the occasional *drip*.

On my return to the lounge I pick up a book, the only thing I can do since the television stopped working a decade ago, and the radio antenna won't pick up a signal unless you take it into the dining room which we can't afford to heat. Or so Dominic told me when I complained the room was starting to smell and black mould spores were beginning to climb the wall surrounding the leaded sash windows.

I glance up at the clock on the mantle, the battery hasn't been replaced since Christmas last. The year he threw the turkey I'd burned onto the lawn for the crows to feast on.

I have to estimate the moments I spend alone by the sky which has been slate grey all day but is now streaked violet above the clouds that are haloed by a sun that looks like an orange that's been dipped in blood.

I put the bookmark on the velvet seat beside me and read the same paragraph twice before my mind wanders fully to thoughts of Dominic.

Not because the hero is romantic but because he's just been accused of cheating on his wife. And the way he reacts to the accusation: deflective and furious reminds me of the way Dominic responded when I asked him what had happened to our wedding photographs.

My skin prickles when I look up and through the glass and see the charcoal and indigo sky, and start to think that maybe the familiar rattle of Dominic's rusty car that billows black smoke from the exhaust as if on fire won't arrive.

I know I rely on him too much but I don't have a choice.

Dominic has never been this late. I've eaten twice today and can tell by the groans my stomach is making it's almost time to make dinner.

I imagine he's had an accident, sped off the road and into a ditch, propelled by the wind into the river, which by the amount and force of the rain that's bouncing off the stoneware planter below the window must be the reason the leak in the loft has become a *drip, splash, drip.*

I put the book down, bending its spine, the front cover glowers at me in accusation, as water sloshes down onto the thin carpet upstairs.

The floorboards groan in protest as I ascend the stairs, ancient and no doubt as rotten as the woodworm-infested grand piano that takes over one half of the drawing room.

I shouldn't, but something compels me – bravery or stupidity, I'm unsure which – to investigate, see if there's anything I can do to patch the roof before the loft caves in. Dominic might shout at me for endangering myself by climbing the rickety ladder but he'll be pleased I took the initiative to prevent further destruction.

I'm hit in the face by a spider's web as my feet land on the wooden slats. The little light emitted from below, through a hole in the floor, is enough to see that crossing over to the other side of the attic is impossible without slipping and breaking an ankle under such sparse light.

There's a fusty smell up here and I'm half-expecting to find a dead bird, my mind conjuring images of a maggot-infested pigeon carcass when something catches my eye. With the moonlight glinting on it's surface it looks like a metal chain. The kind that's kept in the jewellery box in the master bedroom I once hung around my neck and pranced around the room wearing until Dominic saw me from the doorway as he was passing and strode over and ripped it off me, snapping, 'That doesn't belong to you.'

Who the owner of the necklace was and what she meant to Dominic I've never learned. It's just one of many topics of conversation I've been taught to avoid instigating.

I grab the wall and feel with the toes of one socked foot where is safest to walk and shuffle towards the item that leaning over I can see is one of several pieces of silver lying beside a rolled up rug and a pile of clothes.

And then a stained blouse and skirt comes into view as a pair of bright white lights hit the edge of the hole in the roof, illuminating the missing tiles. Two of them. A third broken. The pieces of slate lying beside a full head of . . .

Hair.

I open my mouth to scream but all that comes out is air.

DOMINIC

Then

I was listening to The Pixies on my headphones. The band reminding me of my time in California. The CD bought from my wife's widow's pension. I'd never felt so at home, couldn't imagine where I'd be had I not gone to that casino.

Her late husband's uniform no longer adorned the hook on the back of our bedroom door. The master bed bigger than the room in the hostel I'd been living in before I won the jackpot on that scratch card and took the next flight to Las Vegas. I demanded she remove her dead husband's photo from the bedside though. His image was a daily reminder of her past love. She refused of course. So I trod on it, smiled as I felt the satisfactory crack of the glass beneath the sole of my shoe, saw the scuffmark on the image as I looked down at it. I blamed it on the au pair. Now all that remained of her baby daddy she kept secreted in the back of her head.

I kept the frame though. It was sterling gilt. It was worth five grand according to the pawnbroker. I blamed its disappearance on the 'thieving little cow' she'd employed after sacking the au pair she called a 'clumsy little bitch'.

I took in the antique pine furniture, cut crystal bird, and Royal Dalton figurines. Just the ornaments cost a bomb.

I'd woken up beside her the morning after our first romp to learn just how wealthy she was.

'You're an actress?' I admired the royalty statement in her name from Hallmark she'd left on the nightstand.

'Retired,' she smiled awkwardly at my surprise, popping a pill into her mouth.

I read the label on the bottle of Xanax and decided not to question her about it. The more she swallowed the more pliable she'd be.

She popped another in the taxi on the way to the airport.

'For my nerves,' she said.

I stared at a girl of about seven years old wriggling on her seat opposite us. Next to her sat her bored looking mother who hadn't once, in the hour we'd been waiting, raised her eyes from her magazine to glance in her direction. The girl had hair the same shade as the one in the locket around the neck of the woman beside me, who I'd spent the last three nights with and who pressed her hands together between her knees and inhaled to the count of ten at the advice of her therapist.

'Single Session Cognitive Behavioural Therapy. For my phobia of flying,' she said, the first time I caught her exhaling a whoosh of air.

When the girl noticed me watching her fidget she smiled, showing off dimples and pearly white teeth.

I blinked, at the sound of the PA system declaring, 'Passengers of the 9.15 a.m. flight from Los McCarran International to London Heathrow to board the plane.'

My future wife turned to the window, gazing forlornly at the runway. 'I'm going to miss you.'

'I'm coming with you,' I felt panic rise to my chest, causing it to tighten.

'I wish I could take you home.'

'I'll be seeing you very soon.'

'You will?'

'You didn't think I was going to drop you as soon as we landed did you?'

'Well, I didn't think you'd care to see me again.'

I shot up in my seat, causing a few nosy heads to stir. 'Whatever gave you that idea?'

'I just thought after our fling–'

'Fling?' I barked.

Her eyes flew across the lounge then back to me. 'I just thought a young man like you wouldn't want to lump himself with an old woman like me.'

'Just how old are you?' I laughed nervously.

I knew of course. Had rifled through her handbag, checked the date of birth on her passport and peeked inside her purse to flick through her credit cards as she slept.

'I was late to motherhood. IVF wasn't possible so . . . It all happened so fast. Robert and I wanted to wait until he returned from active duty but then she came along shortly before he was posted to Afghanistan, and of course he didn't return . . .'

I clamped her hands in mine and squeezed them to emphasize the very real fear that burned inside me. 'Take me with you. I can't bear the thought of us being apart.'

I hoped she'd say yes. I had nowhere else to go.

I could tell from her hesitation something was holding her back and when she said, 'You haven't met my daughter yet,' I realised I'd have to fight harder to secure a place inside her heart.

I pushed my bottom lip out and stared down at my feet, not blinking my tired, gritty eyes, so that the ice-cold air conditioning would cause them to water. 'Don't you love me?'

It took her a few seconds to comprehend the meaning behind my words and when she did she brought my hands up to her shoulders and leaned forwards to embrace me.

I held her tight, afraid that if I let go I'd lose her. And I couldn't afford to do that. She was worth too much for me to turn my back on her. Not only could she provide me with a roof over my head and the food to line my stomach with, but also the funds to support the lifestyle I intended to have now that the opportunity had been afforded me.

She took my face in her soft hands, rubbing the day-old stubble that had formed on my cheeks, and gazed longingly into my eyes. 'Mr Reynolds are you proposing to me?'

I'd have been stupid to say no.

KERENSA

Now

My heart is racing as I climb down the ladder on wobbly legs. I fold it against the wall and brush away the dust from the floor below it with a scrape of my foot. I hit the bottom-most step when whoever it is raps aggressively against the front door. I pause and try to figure out who it might be. It can't be my husband, he has a key.

'Don't open the door to anyone, ever,' Dominic told me two years ago. I have never disobeyed him.

'Please, Mrs Reynolds,' Annika says, her desperate voice muffled by the thick oakwood door.

I imagine all kinds of scenarios should Dominic return to find her here making a scene and so, for the first time in my life, I raise the handle as I've seen Dominic do a thousand times, tug it down until I hear the familiar *click*, and pull. It won't open of course. He locked it when he left. There's an emergency key, which he told me only to use under exceptional circumstances such as a fire, 'Not when a parcel is delivered and I'm out.' He'll collect the one that came this morning from the post office in the village tomorrow.

Despite the fact there are no houses nearby, a dog

walker in the woods might see her banging agitatedly on the wood and wonder why.

I unlock Dominic's study to remove the key from the drawer beneath his desk.

An ice-cold trail of uncertainty causes pinpricks of unease to creep across my skin.

I shouldn't have opened the door.

'Mrs Reynolds–' Annika starts before I cut her off with a sharp look.

She's breathless, face etched in scorn. Tall, blonde-haired, blue-eyed, thin and tanned. Her features in direct opposition to my ten-year-old daughter, whose image remains framed inside my head. Except her hair is thicker and slightly darker and her skin is as pale as a porcelain doll's.

'What do you want?' I hiss.

'What is owed me.'

'I owe you nothing.'

'Your husband fired me without notice,' she says irritably, glancing over my shoulder and into the house. 'I want my final lot of wages then I'll leave.'

'He's out.'

She sees the empty space where Dominic's coat usually hangs from the stand in the hall and with a huff shoves her hand into the pocket of her coat to retrieve a bright pink phone, passes it to me, and says, 'Call him.'

I stare down at the phone in my hand.

'What's his number?' she says impatiently, snatching it from me.

'You know he doesn't like to be disturbed when he's running errands.'

'Oh, I know,' she spits.

And I see then why he let her go. She clearly has an issue with authority.

They all have problems. I don't know where he

finds these women. None of them have lasted longer than three months. I thought in Annika we'd found the perfect help. I'm struggling without her. Not that Dominic gave me a choice. I'm grateful he makes the decisions in our marriage but I can't cope with the house-keeping of such a large property as well as the childcare. Thank God for boarding school. Louisa's a handful.

Annika sifts through the bag on her shoulder, pulls out a small pad of paper and a blush pink glittery pen, scribbles something down, rips the page out, and hands it to me. Eleven numbers. 'Call and let me know when to collect my money,' she says in a tone that sounds as hard as the look in her eyes then moves towards the door, stopping just short of opening it, turns back to me and narrows her eyes, 'You know you sit here in your mansion overlooking the sea and you have no idea how much women who aren't as lucky as you struggle to make ends meet. I only hope you never have to worry about keeping the roof over your head and the freezer filled with food. Because without the chance to look for another position and no money in the bank that's the choice I've been left with; pay my rent or eat.'

She tugs open the door, steps out into the harsh wind and slams it shut behind her, causing the painting above the hall table to rattle against the wall. I lunge to stop it before it marks the paintwork, gazing into the eyes of the uniformed gentleman wearing a proud expression on his face that I can never recall the name of.

I lift the frame from the ivory coloured plaster to check – the wall hasn't been nicked – and stare at the numbers on the piece of paper in my hand. I fold it in half, then again, and push it into the half-pocket of my dress.

She's hungry and soon-to-be homeless and there's nothing I can do about it.

I don't have access to money. I've no idea where Dominic keeps it. And even if I did I wouldn't dare go behind his back and give it to her. The last time I did something without his permission he . . .

I shiver from the memory. No Kerensa. Don't go there.

I lock the door and walk down the hall past the kitchen and into Dominic's study to replace the key, dropping it back into the drawer inside his desk as the sound of an unfamiliar engine forces me to hurry.

Before I make it from the room and into the hall there is a trundle of tyres, a driver's door closing and the sound of my husband's voice. But as I near the front door the ear-piercing screech at the side of the house that follows the distant hum of the car exiting the lane stops me from opening it.

Moments later, something is dragged across the gravel. With my ear to the letterbox I can hear huffing and puffing. A car door or boot lid is slammed shut, followed by the rumble of the car Annika drives moving away from the house. I grip the doorframe and stand there like a mannequin.

Seconds pass, turning to minutes, which become ten, then twenty.

What is Dominic doing?

I rush from window to window but can't get a view of whatever it is he's up to out there, dusk has cloaked everything in a thin fog.

I tilt my chin up to the squeal of the garage door being closed twenty minutes after I'd heard it screech open. Too high he'll accuse me of being wilful. Too low and he'll say I'm sulking. I straighten my spine at the metallic clang of something being thrown on the concrete floor inside it. I smile when I hear his footsteps on the stone walkway. I open the door to greet him with a hug of welcome as he raises the shopping bags off the ground, and turn my face to the side to allow him to kiss my cheek as he enters the house, his coarse bristles scouring my soft skin. He drops the loaded bags on the floor and closes the door behind himself, shrugging off his jacket which I take from his outstretched hand and apply to the coat stand while he removes his shoes. I replace them with his slippers, feeling my pulse climb as he sniffs the air.

'You're not cooking,' he says, bringing the bags into the kitchen.

I forgot to defrost the meat, fill a pan with water and drop the ready-chopped vegetables into it in preparation, too distracted by what I found in the attic.

I don't know what compels me to keep Annika's visit from my husband, I certainly don't intend to, and can only hope he didn't pass her on the road, but as soon as I say, 'I was just about to preheat the oven,' it already feels like I've missed the opportunity to tell him she called by.

He gives me a deep look as if searching for something in my expression to pick at, turns his back to me and traipses down the hall.

'Where's your car?'

'Broke down. Had to get a lift back from a passer-by.'

'It's not your day.'

He swings round to face me, frowns.

'There's a leak.'

'Where?'

'The attic.'

'Shit.' He thunders up the stairs, halts midway and stares at the split plasterboard.

I've never heard him swear before. There have been many firsts today, none of them good.

I head for the kitchen while he drags the ladder out and crashes about upstairs.

He returns minutes later, sweating and red-faced. 'I'm going to have to go out to the shed and see if I can find something to cover the hole up with.'

Later, seated opposite one another at the polished mahogany table, listening to our forks scratching against our plates to collect the lasagne, the smacking of our lips as we chew, and the wind down the chimney, I recall what Annika told me shortly after she'd been employed. In hindsight, she was an interfering busybody from the offset.

'Mrs Reynolds,' she cornered me as I exited the kitchen, carrying a glass of water. 'There is something I must speak with you about.'

'What is it?' I said perhaps a little too harshly, for she blinked and took a step back, forcing me to move towards her to hear her whisper.

'You told me your wedding photos were destroyed in a flood.'

'That's right.'

'Only I asked around and searched online and I could find no mention of it anywhere.'

'The river overflowed, swallowed everything on the first floor,' I repeated what Dominic told me, aware that I was rehearsing his words because I felt a need to defend him though I couldn't explain why.

I regret it the moment I do it, but I have the sudden urge to ask Dominic to see them, to gauge his reaction now that some time has passed since I last enquired.

He stabs his fork into a thick slice of pasta. 'I told you. They're gone. Now quit your nagging,' he replies without bothering to look at me. He's never given me cause to doubt him but his inability to catch my eye does exactly that.

My features freeze and my head spins. I can hear a

rush of blood reach my ears as my face warms, and my heart drums so hard against my ribcage I'm convinced Dominic can see the tick in my cleavage.

The water could have damaged them too badly to save. The local media might not have deemed the incident worthy of reporting.

Or Dominic could be lying.

But for what purpose would doing so serve him?

DOMINIC

Then

We held the wedding ceremony in the summerhouse. It meant we didn't have to fork out for a venue or a honeymoon suite in a hotel, and we could head upstairs to bed whenever we wanted. I thought it was cheap and tacky but it wasn't my decision to make. Besides, the more control I let my wife have over the celebration, the easier it would be to blindside her.

Some of the guests were still hanging around the grounds or indoors, queueing to use the downstairs bathroom. We'd left the rear of the property open, pulled the blanketed sofa beds out and parked miniature refrigerators, stocked with snacks and bottled spring water beside them, so that anyone who didn't make it out the front door could stay the night.

My stepdaughter greeted me as I reached the top of the staircase. Stick thin, alabaster skin, huge doe eyes, and a wary look on her face. She creeped me out.

I gave her a wide birth as I side-stepped her and she brought her elbows in to her waist, causing her shoulders to hunch inwards.

I bit the air and she flinched.

I laughed at how easy she was to frighten.

She was a quiet kid, shy, and I knew that once I had

her onside she'd be as loyal and obedient as a dog.

I reached the master bedroom to find my wife passed out on top of the duvet, lying on her side, one arm dangling over the mattress, heels kicked off onto the rug, still dressed. She looked like an English bulldog as she snored, jowls suctioned onto the back of the arm her head was pillowed on, had become hefty in the months since we'd met.

Now I'd married her I was entitled to half her wealth. And once I'd adopted her daughter I'd be put in charge of hers.

KERENSA

Now

I lie awake staring at the ceiling rose, tracing patterns in the webbing cast by the light of the moon filtering through the net curtains Dominic refuses to throw away.

'I don't want anyone to be able to look in,' he said when I suggested washing them.

As if someone might see something they shouldn't while they were drying on the airer. Not that anyone except the postman has ever come close enough to the house to see through the windows for as long as I can remember; since I fell from the headland and tumbled down onto the rocks that create a natural ledge over the Atlantic.

I'd ignored Annika when she'd told me she thought my wedding photos had never existed, pretended not to see the look of astonishment on her face when I'd admitted I couldn't remember them being taken. Another lasting affect of the head injury I sustained from the fall. But I can't deny what I've seen with my own two eyes.

Whose wig is it in our attic?

I've read enough Agatha Christie novels to know she must have meant something to Dominic. You don't hide a living persons belongings unless having them visible upsets you. And by the style of the clothing the material must be at least twenty years old.

Long before my accident. So they can't be mine.

I turn my head towards my husband whose eyes are wide open, causing me to gasp.

He smiles and reaches out to me. I let his hand slip between my legs.

'What would you do without me?' he asked, as I lay in my hospital bed with a concussion.

He pays for the shopping and goes out to buy it. I can't even drink from any of the bone china cups hooked onto the Welsh dresser without spilling the liquid contained within it down my front. The one-sided tremor another symptom of my clifftop descent.

My answer remains the same.

'I only remember my life with you.'

'Maybe that's a good thing,' he said.

'Why, were you a bit of a rogue?'

'Don't tell me you've never sinned?' he said with a mischievous glint in his eyes.

'I haven't,' I wanted to say, but I couldn't be sure.

DOMINIC

Then

The process of adoption was fairly straightforward. I had to show the social worker who came out to meet me my driving licence as a form of identification and my copy from the Disclosure And Barring Service to prove I was clean of offences, to ensure it matched the one they'd already received. We spoke for about an hour. She wanted to know about my childhood, my parenting style, and what I did for a living.

I told her what I knew she'd want to hear. That my parents were loving and caring, if a little over-protective (no one's perfect, and I knew that adding in some negatives would make my story more believable) and provided a warm, safe, financially stable environment for me.

'No brothers or sisters?' she asked.

'No siblings.' When her face dropped I added, 'All the better for me though. I had double cuddles, as my late mum used to say.'

She smiled at this. Then her mouth shaped into an 'O'. She squinted, said in a patronizing tone, 'She's no longer around then?'

I shook my head. 'Passed away a couple of years ago.'

She tilted her head to the side, pressed her lips together into a sad smile and nodded, and I had to inhale a deep breath to calm the impulse to lunge forward and slap her.

I grit my teeth, took my soon-to-be adopted daughter's hand in mine, and added, 'And to answer your other questions I'm of the belief that kids need attention and independence. They should be nurtured while given the responsibility to develop their autonomy.'

I'd read in a psychology textbook in the downstairs library that if you supplied vague answers to intrusive questions you neither supplied the respondent with a positive or negative reply.

'And in answer to your third, I work in a betting shop at the moment, though it's purely for the income. I'm not a gambling man.'

I did visit the bookies every day, though she couldn't know I was spending my future inheritance there.

That seemed to please her as she closed her notebook and shook my hand. 'We'll write to you both,' she said, nodding to my wife who appeared in the doorway as I stood to escort the social worker out. She was glassy-eyed and muted with Vicodin. She'd had her interview the week before.

I walked the social worker to the door, and exhaled a sigh of relief once it was closed behind her.

When I returned to the lounge I found it empty, my soon-to-be adopted stepdaughter's small footsteps treading up the staircase.

I entered the kitchen to find my wife searching the cupboard for the pill bottle.

She'd doubled her dose since I'd moved in, carrying my only possessions in the rucksack I'd brought on the flight back from the US.

Grinding one up and adding it to her morning coffee, which she used to swallow one, had seen to that. She was easier to manipulate that way.

KERENSA

Now

Dominic's back in the attic re-patching the hole in the insulation he reckons birds have stolen overnight to help build their nests.

'I covered this up as best I could. Whatever got through it has teeth like a shark,' he calls down.

I know from the sound of his footsteps he's nowhere near the missing tiles where he used a staplegun to fix a square of tarpaulin to four footlong pieces of wood he marched up the ladder with last night, holding a small torch between his teeth to see where he was going, once the rain had stopped.

I think he's trying to find out if any of the things I found yesterday – which he has to pass to reach the gap in the roof – have been damaged by the rainwater.

I stand below the hatch, holding the ladder. 'Are you working today?'

'Why are you interested?' he calls down.

'I just wondered how you were going to get there without your car.'

'Can't you see I've got more important things to deal with?'

'Of course. But don't you need the money?'

'I've got plenty of that.' He laughs.

Have you? I wouldn't know because I've not seen any since . . .

A memory smacks me in the face.

I'm opening a green wallet. It's heavy and the coins inside it tinkle as I remove a wedge of folded notes and stuff them into the heel of my sock so I can feel the lump they make when I slide my foot into my trainers.

Why?

DOMINIC

Then

While her mother slept upstairs – something she did most afternoons once the sedative effect of the drugs she took with her lunchtime gin and tonic had kicked in, leaving her slurring her words and incapable of performing the most basic of household tasks – I took my waiflike stepdaughter with me to the supermarket. On the way back we stopped for ice-cream and she began to open up to me about her feelings towards her useless, pill addict mother.

'I wish she'd take me to the beach like she used to.'

'What did you get up to there?'

'Race across the sand, collect crabs in buckets from the rockpools, paddle in the sea, eat salty chips on the promenade . . .'

'Let's go then.'

'Really?' her eyes lit up.

'Sure.'

After I let her 'win' the race, build the best sandcastle, collect the biggest crab we could find – which I assured her meant she'd won the *who can collect the most crabs?* challenge – and had convinced her to get her hair wet by swimming as far out into the Atlantic as she could without getting swept away by the tide, I knew I'd gained her trust. And when I told her I understood how she must be feeling abandoned by her mother since I'd come on the scene and assured her she would be no longer I knew I'd earned myself a brownie point that I could use to my advantage any time I wanted.

Then we returned home to find the dirty dishes still piled high next to the draining board, her mother dismissing her daughter's excited chatter about our bonding session with a wave of her hand, too entranced by The Real Housewives of some American State she was watching on the television, and I realised I didn't need to turn her against her mother, the lazy woman was doing a grand enough job of alienating her daughter without my input.

KERENSA

Now

I watch the trees sway in the wind, their boughs creaking, as a rush of wind funnels into the room.

The gale has been howling down the chimney that leads through the fireplace and into our bedroom all night, blowing debris across the worn carpet. Which I had to kneel on the floor to scoop into a paper bag and deposit into the kitchen bin. It's cold enough for a fire but lighting one would be suicide.

I recall the last sentence from the book I was reading yesterday before my concentration began to wane, the roaring wind too interruptive to ignore.

The scent of burning wood crackling on a cold winter's night as you gaze into the dancing flames.

'Why can't we light the fire? They're so romantic,' I sigh.

'If you want to suffocate on noxious fumes,' Dominic replies. 'The chimney hasn't been swept in years.'

Dominic has never spent so much time at home, at least not for the last twenty-four months, which is as far back as my memory will go. He told me that he works in a betting shop as a bookie. But his boss must be annoyed because he hasn't called in sick. And he's being far more watchful of my movements than usual.

He paces and wrings his hands and fiddles with the loose button on his shirt.

We had a phone once. A cream one with a curled cable. I remember how the hard plastic felt as I held it between the right-hand-side of my face and shoulder.

'Have you called a roofer?'

His button pops off and knocks my beaker over, sending a spray of water across the table. Eyes blazing with fury he stomps towards me.

Inches from my face I can feel his hot breath on the bridge of my nose.

'You think I'm incompetent? That I can't fix it myself? That I need a woman to tell me what to do? Did I ask for your opinion?'

Spine slamming against the back of the dining chair, mouth too dry to speak, I can only shake my head which is tilted so far back it hurts my neck.

His shoulders drop an inch and the tick above his left eyebrow stops on cue as the doorbell chimes.

He takes a step back and exits the room not once retracting his eyes from mine.

I can't see him but I recognise his accent. 'Franc Borkowski. Annika's brother.'

'How can I help you?' Dominic says.

'She didn't return home yesterday.'

'She doesn't work for us anymore.'

'She came here though. She borrowed my car.'

I always thought it was her own.

I can tell by his hesitation that Dominic is worried.

'Yes, she spoke to my wife.'

A lead-weighted stone forms in my chest and drops to my stomach.

Even if Annika passed Dominic while he was being

driven home he couldn't know that we'd talked.

'She came to collect her final month's wages.'

How does he know the reason for her visit without having overheard our conversation?

'You gave it her?'

'In full,' Dominic affirms.

When?

Had he withdrew the money intending to meet her here and, late because his car had broken down they'd stopped their cars to exchange the money when they passed each other on the road?

If they had originally planned to meet here it would explain why Annika appeared frustrated when she learned that he was out.

'How much?'

'Eight hundred pounds.'

'That's not enough.'

'Twenty pounds an hour,' Dominic says, sounding offended.

'I mean to disappear with.'

'You think she's left town?' Dominic says, a tell-tale hint of relief having entered his voice. 'I suppose it depends on how much money she has on her.'

'She's living with me because her landlord kicked her out for failing to pay her rent because she couldn't afford it.'

'Did she tell you why we had to let her go?'

'No.'

'She turned up stinking of booze.'

No she didn't.

'My wife caught her crying in the bathroom. She'd forgotten to lock the door.'

That never happened.

'Her eyes were permanently glazed as though she was doped up on something and her work was shoddy at best.'

'She doesn't drink.'

'She did that day.'

'What day?'

'The day I fired her.'

'She can't drink.'

'Alcohol problem? It's common in your country isn't it?'

'What is?'

'Vodka. That's what the Polish drink, isn't it?'

'She's allergic.'

'To what?'

'Alcohol.'

'Is that what you call addiction these days?'

'My sister is missing an enzyme, preventing her liver from metabolizing methanol. Look it up. I came here to find out when you'd last seen her. If she'd said anything to you that might give the police some idea of her state of mind or that could tell us where she might be. I'm not going to stand here and listen to you badmouth her.'

'The police?' Dominic says with alarm.

'I had to get a taxi to work today. That's how I know something's happened to her. She wouldn't have taken my car if she was going to–'

'Drive into the river.'

'Take off somewhere without telling anyone where she was going,' he says through gritted teeth.

'Which appears to be exactly what she's done.'

Annika's brother murmurs something then the door *clicks* closed and I hear him retreat. Seconds later, there's a scuffle, some shouting – though I can't make out what's being said as their voices are carried away on the wind – and I run to the window in the lounge. There's no sign of him. He must have begun his walk home along the coastal path. He's brave, the weather's not ideal.

I think about Dominic's comment to Franc and how sure he sounded when he told the man his sister had likely driven into the river. Dominic and Annika would both have had to pass the river on their way here. All that separates it from the road is a metre-wide verge. I caught a glimpse of it through the trees on our way back from the hospital.

'I recommend she returns for her weekly physiotherapy sessions and I've made a referral to a neuro-psychologist to help with the amnesia,' the doctor said, before discharging me into the care of the husband I didn't recognise.

We never saw him again.

When I queried the letter that came through the door a month later Dominic told me it must have been posted to us by mistake. The address didn't match the one he'd given the doctor before I'd been released and driven to this house.

'Electricity bill,' he said, scooping it up off the mat.

After six months I stopped expecting Dominic to open the envelope to reveal the letter on headed NHS paper, bearing the time and date of my appointment.

I taught myself how to walk without a wobble and to stretch my limbs as soon as I woke to prevent my muscles from stiffening up from lack of use.

Dominic put a stop to me walking up and down the stairs, blaming his migraines on the sound of my echoing feet. But when I offered him advice on how to manage them he shouted: 'You're the headache, now shut up and get the dinner on.'

I know he comes across as patriarchal, old-fashioned, sexist even. And that I'm dependent on him due to my long-term health conditions which make me vulnerable. But until now, I didn't resent him for it.

I picked up a book from the downstairs library not long after I came here (I still can't think of myself as returning because it didn't feel like home). It was titled The Actor's Guide to Character Illness, and was initialled inside to M. H. I wanted to learn more about the damage sustained during a traumatic head injury. I read that the resulting loss of oxygen in certain areas of the brain can result in a myriad of neurological dysfunction. And that memory loss cannot always be improved by exercising the mind. Something I determined to prove wrong.

So while I can't recall how I learned to read I tried to use my skill to do so to stretch my short-term memory. I can remember as far back as waking up in a hospital bed, fourteen days before Dominic took me home. Everything prior to that is a blank screen like the one on the dusty television.

The door slamming shut causes me to jump in fright.

I turn towards Dominic just as he enters the room, hair windswept, cheeks pinched with the cold, a little out of breath, knees grass-stained, shoes clotted in mud.

'What have you done?'

DOMINIC

Then

My wife lay on the chaise longue staring out at the waves crashing against the jagged rocks below the third floor bay window. She looked washed-out and bored. I'd plied her with compliments to sooth her over-indulgent soul but she was still upset, and her self-pity was becoming tedious.

'I'm a hash-been. No one wants to employ me anymore so I shut myshelf away in this big old houshe, neglecting my family . . .'

'You're drunk, again.'

'Sho what if I am? No one caresh.'

'You're just feeling sorry for yourself.'

'Sho would you be if you had lost your looksh and your career.'

She did this every day, once she'd had her fill of booze and analgesia. I was tired, had let my guard down, and this time instead of placating her I did something she wasn't expecting.

'All right, fine, you are a wrinkly woman whose breath tastes like sour grapes and ash. Is that what you want me to say?'

She laughed bitterly then pitched her pillow at my head. It took all my restraint not to smother her with it. But it wouldn't do me any good to lose my temper.

'I'm taking our daughter to the park while you sleep off your foul attitude.'

I didn't stop and turn when I heard a thump behind me. Either she'd fallen out the bed or had thrown one of the glass paperweights she collected on the built-in, nineties style shelving unit surrounding it at me. I couldn't give a toss either way.

The girl had been filling out since I'd been spending most of my time fashioning her.

'How do I look Daddy?' she spun on her new sparkling silver shoes.

'Hmmm, too grown up. Lose the lipstick. Where did you get it from anyway?'

'I stoled it from Mum's dressing table. She didn't notice.'

I stormed towards her, pulled a handkerchief from the pocket inside my chinos and wiped the painted smile off her face, leaving her lips and chin raw.

'There, now you don't look like a whore.'

'What's a whore?'

I lunged forward causing her to jump backwards, smacking the back of her head against the wall. 'Don't ever say that word again, you're nothing like my mother!'

I shook off the memory of the bitch who'd birthed me. Had left me in a dirty nappy, crying to be fed while she fucked the paedos – who used to enter my bedroom after she'd passed out, while I hid beneath the bed shaking – for the money to buy her booze.

Women are fickle. Give them a yarn of wool and they'll soon tie themselves up with their desire to be loved.

'Let's look at you,' I said, studying her fearful features. 'Dry your eyes and quit frowning, it makes you look ugly.'

KERENSA

Now

He crinkles his nose at me, 'What do you mean, *what have I done?*'

'To Franc, just now. It sounded like you were fighting.'

He looks like he wants to kill me and I'm sure he would given half the chance but he regains control of his senses as he raises his hand.

He's never hit me before. At least not that I can remember.

He swipes a wet leaf from his lapel.

'Annika's gone missing.'

'I heard.'

He glances from me to the window, stomps towards it and snaps the curtains closed with so much force he almost tears the curtain pole off its brackets.

'How did you know Annika stopped by?'

He pulls a tiny piece of paper from his trouser pocket and unfolds it to display Annika's mobile phone number.

I instinctively pat the half-pocket above my right hip on the dress I'm wearing even though I know it's in the wash, my fingers brushing against the pocketless denim one I have on.

I feel my face warm as my panic-stricken pulse rises. I try to swallow the lump forming in my throat, lick my lips to moisten them, and ignore the wild strumming of my heartbeat against my ribcage.

'I found this on the bedroom floor.'

'How did you know what she came here for?'

'I planned to meet her here.'

A snake of ice-cold dread slithers down my spine and my vision blurs.

'When?'

'The evening she came to collect her final lot of wages.'

'Where?'

'Out front. She was stood leaning against her car parked on the driveway when I arrived.'

I heard two cars after she left the house. The one that must have been driven by the person who gave Dominic a lift home. Arriving and leaving in less than a minute. And Annika's soon after. So why did it take Dominic twenty minutes to walk through the front door? And what had he been doing in the garage?

Unless the scream of the garage door opening was really that of a female's cry for help.

'I forgot she came over, sorry.'

'You will be.'

DOMINIC

Then

The less attention her mother gave her, the more time the girl spent with me, in the lounge playing Monopoly, watching Disney films, and eating the snacks I filled the delicately painted bowls with. A wedding gift to the wife and her ex-husband I later discovered, which led to their demise.

She seemed to be making more of an effort to socialise too, had begun to make friends with some of the kids who lived nearby.

She knocked the ball into the hedge and ran past me, diving into the bush to fetch it. Her eyes sparkled when she laughed; a high-pitched cackle, like a witch.

She'd sure as hell put a spell on the boy she'd coaxed into making her a den.

And the boy's mother. With a bun fixed up on her head, legs bare like the first day I'd laid eyes on her, she looked like Anna Kournikova. She smelled of rosewater and her bronzed skin shone in the sun. I couldn't stop thinking about ripping her knickers off with my teeth.

When she noticed me staring at her she'd stare right back, challenging me to a contest of wills there was no chance she'd win. Not when she paraded around the garden with a bat, chasing after the tennis ball that had ran off-course, in those skimpy shorts that barely covered her arse. She had me wanting to wrap her legs round mine when she batted those long eyelashes at me.

She reminded me of a girl I once knew.

But I had a good thing going, I couldn't ruin it.

KERENSA

Now

He takes my shaking hand in his before I can snatch it away.

The way the sparse lighting shadows his features causes his eye colour to darken like two pieces of coal.

He coils his hand round my wrist unleashing a memory.

I know something I shouldn't and it's going to get me killed, so I'm stuffing bank notes beneath the heel of my socked foot to aid my escape. But who I'm running from or why I hadn't known, till now.

'It was you.'

He blinks.

'What are you talking about?'

'You did something . . . and I . . . I wanted to get away from you . . . I tried to leave, and . . . you wouldn't let me.'

'I had no choice, Kerensa.'

'You do now.'

He shakes his head.

'It's too late. You've got to go.'

'G– go where?'

DOMINIC

Then

I'd just tucked our daughter in, read her a bedtime story, was closing the door behind me when I glanced down and noticed my flies were undone. My wife was entering our bedroom, had turned and saw me pulling the zip of my jeans up.

'Oh, how could you?' she shrieked.

'What? No! It's not what you think.'

'Don't try to gaslight me.'

'Those pills you take have addled your brain.'

'Pervert.'

'You've got this entire situation wrong.' I grabbed her as she flew past me.

She twisted her arm, forcing me to let go of her sleeve.

'I know what it looks like but I assure you I would never–'

'Don't even think of denying it,' she said, snivelling into a tissue.

'You're paranoid. She's my daughter!'

'No she's not!'

My blood boiled, my pulse rose, and my hands formed into fists at my sides.

She pushed her nose into my face so I could feel her

furious hot breath on my chin. 'You do so much as lay a hand on *my* daughter and I'll take her and leave,' she said.

She turned and stormed across the room, towards the bedroom door I'd kicked shut so our daughter wouldn't hear us argue above the sound of the piano concerto playing from the downstairs speakers. I raced after her, caught her by the hair, wrapped a bunch of it round my fist and tugged on it, forcing her head back and her eyes to widen in shock.

'Don't threaten me,' I spat.

I'd expected to find fear in them but instead her eyes blazed with something like lust. At least that's how I'd describe it.

'You're enjoying this aren't you?' I didn't give her time to reply, pressing my other hand against her throat. 'You want it rough really, don't you?'

She opened her mouth and croaked out a sob, so, releasing my hold enough to allow her to inhale a breath of air, I dragged her to the dressing table and threw her down on the polished wood.

'You all do. Though none of you'll ever admit you like it when a man takes charge. It goes against your feminist ideals.'

She exhaled a breathy cry of pleasure right before I wrapped my hand round her throat and squeezed it tight.

'You say you don't like it when a man takes control but your body betrays you in the way that it responds.'

Her face went purple as she struggled to escape my grip, eyes bulging, limbs slackening as she released a little sigh of surrender.

'If anyone's perverted, it's you.'

KERENSA

Now

I've convinced myself that boredom will kill me sooner than he will.

It has only been a few hours since Dominic dumped me on the floor that stinks of mildew. I've already searched the room for a way out and now my adrenalin has worn off, my throat is dry, my voice hoarse, and I can't stop shivering.

Yawning, I leaf through a box of scripts I find lodged under a wooden chest filled with dank smelling dolls. His daughter's? I read them because I've got nothing else to do. One is for a play about a woman whose neighbour gaslights her until she goes mad. There's another for a television drama about a middle-aged woman whose husband cheats on her with her best friend who just happens to be the manager of a psychiatric hospital where she has her admitted, enabling her to shack up with her lover.

They're all sad stories about family members betraying each other or lying to one another. Quite fitting I suppose, considering my circumstances.

I can see how hunger, thirst, loneliness and isolation can be used to emotionally torture someone but when it grows dark I realise my true battle has only just begun.

The window panes rattle, the cracked joists groan overhead, and my stomach complains as my eyelids droop and I succumb to exhaustion.

I awake sometime post-dawn to the sound of birds flapping about on the opposite side of the wall, and the hot water pipes vibrating under my stiff arm and numb foot.

I stand to walk off the pins and needles and yelp as a shadow the height and width of a man moves away from the cabinet to my left.

'You scared me.'

The expression on Dominic's face tells me this pleases him.

'I've brought you something to eat and drink,' he says, cocking his head towards the tray on the floor.

The food looks like it's been fermenting on the plate for a while. He must have been sitting watching me sleep for ages.

'Not hungry?'

I stare at him until he shrugs.

He lands on the floor with a loud smack, crosses his legs and balances the plate on his lap to tuck into my meal.

To prove he hasn't poisoned it?

He eats the two slices of buttered toast slathered in strawberry jam and slurps the glass of orange juice as though *his* stomach has been growling all night.

'You can't keep me here forever.'

He swallows his last mouthful and wipes the crumbs from his mouth with the napkin. 'I don't intend to.'

DOMINIC

Then

'Daddy?' I heard from behind me.

I turned. The door was open a crack. The noise we were making had disguised the sound of her footfall padding along the hall to unlatch the door.

I shot her a look that caused her lip to quiver. 'Get out!'

She spun round and darted down the hall to the nursery.

Her mother lay slack-featured on her side, hair covering her doughy complexion.

I pulled the duvet up to cover her bruised neck.

KERENSA

Now

He brings me meals three times a day but I'm not stupid. I know he's trying to drug me, make me compliant to whatever it is he wants from me. It can't be sexual. I've never refused him. I let him do what he wants to me because I like it. I don't know if there was ever a time I didn't, my preferences lost to me.

We don't need a safe word, I get off on being told what to do, I get a kick out of displeasing him, I enjoy the satisfied grunts he makes while he's punishing me. Our sex life has always been thrilling.

From the very first day I walked through the front door he was nothing but chivalrous and kind, cooking, catering to my every need, and so one night as he lay beside me I reached out for him, let him pull me towards him and envelop my waist as he brought me above him and crushed me against his solid chest.

I felt anchored in a stormy sea and panicked when he wasn't around. I grew to yearn his companionship, his touch.

Now I am lost. Like a goldfish that's been flung into the ocean.

There is no way out. I've searched. No windows, nothing to break the doors down with. Nothing to smash over his head. Not that I'd have the energy to fight him.

Perhaps that's why he's doing this; to weaken me. It's working, I'm exhausted.

DOMINIC

Then

I found her in the playhouse, curled up at the back, behind the toy washing machine. I crept in beside her, drew her towards me. She was shaking.

'What's wrong?'

She gave a little whimper and tried to prise my arms off her.

'Mum was crying.'

'She's sleeping.'

'She sounded upset.'

'It was just a scaremare.'

'Did you kiss her better?'

'Sure.'

She shuddered.

'It's bed time. You've got to be up early in the morning. You need to sleep.'

She nodded. I released her but she wrapped her arms round my neck so I lifted her up and carried her out of the playhouse on my back.

She laughed when I growled and prowled from the room, her earlier fright a memory.

The tension in my muscles receded, my earlier aggression forgotten.

KERENSA

Now

Time never meant anything before but now I have no idea when daylight is so I doze for a while then lie awake for a few more, alternately throwing up bile and gripping my tight stomach which cramps now I can no longer pee. It's been so long since I consumed liquid my body is failing.

That's it. That's how I can get out of here.

I lie very still, facing the floor, practising how to breathe with minimal movement of my chest. I perfect it just a few unknown minutes before the sound of Dominic's footsteps treading heavily up the stairs threatens to send my pulse sky-rocketing, giving me away.

DOMINIC

Then

She looked peaceful, her eyelids flickered as she slept. I wondered what she dreamed about, if I ever entered them. I watched her chest rise and fall for a minute, maybe more. Once I was satisfied she wouldn't wake I crept backwards from the room and bolted the door behind me.

I watched my footing on the creaky board below the carpet as I entered my bedroom.

Morvoren's face had taken on a waxy appearance in the hours since I'd been gone. There was a sheen of sweat above her mouth and a pool of urine below her fat arse.

She was a dead weight. Too heavy to carry to the car to dispose of elsewhere, I realised, once I'd wrapped her in the duvet like a sausage roll and dragged her corpse from the room. I stood at the top of the staircase, craned my neck and took in a lungful of shit-stained air – she was leaking bodily fluids from every orifice – and spotted the loft hatch.

It'll do for now. Somewhere to keep her until I can hire an electric saw.

Chopping her into pieces and wrapping each dismembered part up in refuse liners was the only way I was going to be able to get her down the stairs. Then all I had to do was find a good place, far away from here, to bury her.

KERENSA

Now

He enters the room, making sure to lock the door behind him before stepping over the mess cluttering the floor to seek me out.

He sits beside me to check my pulse, which is as erratic as my heartbeat now my blood sugar levels are all out of whack.

I play dead for as long as I can stand while he talks incessantly about falling for the girl next door, who did not reciprocate the love he felt for her.

I could be dreaming. This can't be real.

He's gone cuckoo.

'She was my only friend . . . kids my age couldn't see past the dirt on my scruffy, undersized hand-me-down clothes . . . my hair stank of cigarettes . . . her mum kept a roof over their head with a wedding ring while mine chose to whore herself to a different man every night, not that there's any difference . . .'

He leans over me, strokes my hair, twirls a lock of it round his finger, sniffs it, then leaves.

I don't move until I'm sure he hasn't crept back up the stairs to catch me out. That's when I realise I didn't hear him lock the door.

DOMINIC

Then

Wearing a pair of gloves, I filled my wife's most-used handbag with her purse, keys, and phone, drove to one of the smaller train stations that had no cameras, and left it beneath a seat on the sleeper heading for Bristol Temple Meads.

I practised what to say to the police on the drive to the station. I parked round the corner so that by the time I got there I was panting and my eyes were watering from the cold. I was introduced by the desk sergeant to a PC Trelore who had a Cornish accent as thick as his ginger beard.

'Wha can I help you with sire?'

'My wife has gone missing.'

'I see.' He turned towards the woman typing furiously on the desktop computer with her eyes on the door rather than the screen in front of her and said, 'We'll be in room two.'

She nodded without turning to look at me. It was then I realised she didn't need to. There was a camera above her head aimed directly at us, and on another screen to her left a view of all the CCTV images from the other cameras spread throughout the building.

I followed the filth inside the white-painted room

with scuffmarks on the door and another camera centred above the table where two seats were parked opposite one another at either side of it.

He sat. I remained standing. I wanted to appear restless and worried.

He tilted his head to the chair. 'Take a seat Mr?'

'Reynolds. Dominic.'

'My name is Constable Trelore,' he said, emphasising the 'r'. 'Can you tell me why you're here?'

I thought he might be stupid then realised he was doing this because we were being recorded and he wanted me to repeat what I'd just told him. 'My wife has gone.'

'When did you notice she was missing?'

'This morning.'

'This morning.'

Why was he paraphrasing me?

'I woke up and she wasn't there.'

'You woke up in bed where?'

'Cliffside, the house on the–'

'I know the one. Nice place. What's your wife's name?'

'Morvoren.'

'And how old is M–'

'Does it matter?' His calmness was irritating. 'Shouldn't you be out there looking for her?'

'Mr Reynolds, I need a description of your wife before I send my colleagues in the Missing Persons Team out looking for her.'

'She's fifty.'

'Do you have a photograph of her?'

'No. I . . . I didn't think.'

'It doesn't matter. I'll have one of my colleagues collect one from you. I suspect you have plenty of them back at the house?'

'She was an actress. I'm sure there are lots online

you could use.'

He looked disappointed and I wondered if the picture was an excuse to come snooping round my home.

'We need a recent one.'

He leaned forward over the notepad he was writing everything I said down on as the sun peeked out from behind a cloud, leaving a pool of light on the table. 'When was the last time you saw Morvoren?'

'She went up to bed before me. Said she was feeling tired. It was about 9 p.m.'

'Is that usual?'

'Yes. She's always been that way. Early to bed early to rise. I suspect it's the pills she takes.'

'She's on medication?'

'Xanax. Vicodin. There may be others but they're the only ones I know the names of.'

'Hmmm, they're unusual in the UK. Who prescribes them to her?'

'I'm not sure. I assumed it was a private doctor, you know? She used to travel to London a lot.'

'Used to?'

Shit. Freudian slip.

'I mean, she doesn't drive anymore so she hasn't gone there for a while.'

Technically true since prior to her death she was too pissed to get behind the steering wheel and I'm now in possession of her car.

'You don't take her?'

'No. She hasn't asked.'

'So how does she get hold of her medication now?'

'I . . . I'm not sure exactly.'

'Do you know what she takes them for? I'm assuming she suffers from anxiety as that's what Xanax is used to treat and Vicodin is an analgesic so I'm guessing she is in some amount of pain.'

'I'm sorry, I've never asked. It seemed a bit intrusive, you know?'

'What time did you wake up?'

'8 a.m. That's when my alarm goes off.'

'And where would Morvoren usually be at this time?'

'Eating breakfast, on the phone, getting our daughter ready for school . . .'

'And where is she now?'

'If I knew that I wouldn't be here would I?'

'Your daughter, Mr Reynolds.'

'Oh, right, I see, yes, sorry. She's with the . . . nanny. Well, she's more of a cleaner really.'

'An au pair?'

'Uh-huh.'

'I'm going to need to speak to her.'

'My daughter?'

'Yes, her as well. But I mean the au pair. What's her name?'

'Uh . . .'

I had to think fast to come up with one.

'And how has your wife been recently? Has she been preoccupied for instance or has she appeared out of sorts in any way?'

'She's been drinking more than usual.'

'And how much does she usually drink, Mr Reynolds?'

'Gin's her tipple. She likes a glass for lunch, another mid-afternoon, then tends to down a couple in the evening, hence the reason she hasn't driven the car recently.'

'Hmmm, so more than the recommended daily allowance then?'

'I suppose so, yes.'

'Where is it now, the car?'

'Here.'

'Did you notice anything missing from the house?'

'No.'

'She hasn't taken anything with her.'

'I don't know. I mean, I haven't looked. I didn't think it was relevant.'

'Not to worry. You can check while I delegate someone to drive over to the house to collect a photograph of Morvoren from you.'

He gave me a weak commiserating smile.

'Any idea where your wife might have gone? Any errands she had to run today she may have forgotten to tell you about? Any friends nearby she could have gone to visit?'

'No, not that I can think of. She doesn't really go out anymore.'

'And why is that?'

Because she's dead.

'A lot of her friends are in the industry, you know. Actresses, models, singers. Most of them are still employed so they're working or on tour. They have such busy schedules they don't seem to be able to find the time to meet up with her anymore. And then there's the house.'

I didn't want him speaking to Lizette. The one she was with the day I met her in the casino.

'The house.'

'She likes a clean home, has always been very organised. Since her retirement–'

'Retired? That's unusual isn't it, for someone her age, I mean.'

'Yes, I suppose it is, but after her husband died she . . . I think she had some kind of breakdown from the grief. Stepped down from her career. I know she let go an offer to appear in a new adaptation of that film. What's it called?' I drummed my temple. '*Désirée's Dalliance*. A spoof of–'

'Désirée's Baby.'

'That's right.'

I knew that when he Googled the plot on IMDB he'd see that instead of walking into a swamp with her illegitimate infant, the married woman, consumed with shame takes her own life after her husband discovers her affair with another man. I wanted to make him think, draw his own hypothesis as to what he believed might have happened to my wife.

I'd also bought two unregistered payphones, had sent several text messages between the two from thirty miles apart. In them I'd alluded to an affair. When the police eventually decided to search the house they'd find hers secreted inside a shoebox at the bottom of her wardrobe.

It was almost midday by the time I returned to the house to find my daughter sat at the dining table, wearing her school uniform – the cardigan inside out – eating from a bowl of cereal drowning in milk.

I thought about what I'd told PC Trelore, caught off-guard by the possibility of him discovering I'd left our daughter at home alone and wondered how quickly I could employ an au pair, convince her to use the name I'd given her, the first to enter my mind because it belonged to the only girl who'd ever stolen my heart, and lie to the police about how long she'd worked for us.

KERENSA

Now

I tip-toe to the door, twist the knob until it opens, turn left and traipse the pitch ebony passageway. The door at the end opens with ease. The room is filled with cabinets fit to burst, boxes of paper, and among them I find a birth certificate with the date of birth Dominic gave me when I asked him how old I was and where I'd been born, making me twenty-six.

The child's and parent's names are illegible. The ink has run and the paper disintegrates between my fingers. There's an adoption certificate too but the only name on it that's visible is Dominic's.

DOMINIC

Then

It was never my intention to kill my wife. She was far more valuable to me alive. I couldn't access her life insurance policy until she'd been declared legally dead. The property had been left in her daughter's name, which she couldn't sell until she turned eighteen. So all we had to live off were the expensive pieces of furniture and antiques I sold from the house, and once the police realised I was cashing her royalty cheques in the Money Shop they would stop the payments. But when she accused me of the very thing that had marred my childhood, the red mist had descended, and I'd acted on impulse. The urge too powerful to avoid. And now I was stuck with her brat, struggling to make ends meet as she racked up further items I had to buy her: a rabbit, ballet classes, a school trip, violin lessons, and on it went. I had to find another source of income– fast.

'I don't have a never-ending money pot, you know.'

She was seated at the back of the car playing Sonic on her Nintendo Switch.

'Hey! Are you listening to me?'

She threw her games console to the side and folded her arms across her stiff waist. It slid off the seat and skidded beneath the footwell as I turned a sharp corner.

'You should be grateful. I never had toys or went to school. I didn't have the opportunity to learn how to play musical instruments or own a bike to go out riding with my mates.'

'That's sad.'

'Yes, it is.'

She couldn't comprehend what it was like because she'd been brought up without a care in the world, the realities of life would hit her full pelt once she realised it didn't revolve around her.

The traffic slowed as we reached the junction, jammed between a Vauxhall and a Renault that had stopped so close I couldn't do a U-turn.

'You may as well walk from here. It's only a quarter of a mile. You don't have any roads to cross.'

'Mum used to park right outside.'

'Well, your mum's not here anymore, and this is my car now. I'm not stopping on double yellows. I can't afford a fine.'

'It's raining.'

'Put your hood up.'

She turned her nose up at me and stared out of the window.

I could feel my hand itching to wipe the smirk off her face.

We arrived at the school fifteen minutes late. I could feel the heat of my anger rising to the surface of my skin when she made no move to leave the car.

'What are you waiting for?'

She leaned over the centre console and held out her hand. 'Dinner money.'

'I've made you a packed lunch.'

'I don't like cheese.'

'Why didn't you tell me that before I put it in your

sandwich?' I spoke between gritted teeth.

She gave me a blank stare.

I leaned my hand back and opened the door but she just tipped her head back and gave me that dead-eyed stare I'd become accustomed too that said 'I'm not listening to you, you're not my dad.' Despite the fact I was the only one she'd ever known.

'Get out the car!'

Her eyes widened and two parents exiting the playground gave me a dirty look.

I hadn't meant to lose my temper, and knew that doing so in public would only demonstrate to everyone who already held me accountable that I had the ammunition to get rid of my wife, which I didn't need while the old bill were breathing down my neck.

I had to play the long game if I wanted access to the fortune that was owed me.

'I'm sorry I shouted at you. I'm upset and . . . here.' I handed her my last tenner.

She beamed.

I had to admit defeat. I needed help. I couldn't balance the chores and take care of a child while maintaining the façade of a distraught husband and father. Besides, it would go in my favour if I didn't appear to be coping so well.

KERENSA

Now

There's a rustling from the eaves. The birds have pecked and gnawed their way through the wood and made themselves at home inside the loft space again. I return to my spot on the floor of the room he forgot to lock and reposition myself as before.

He returns some time later with a tray of food. He knows I've moved, can sense the disturbance in the air. Either that or he can see the dust moats floating gently back down to settle on the surfaces of the furniture and ornaments, can hear my shallow breaths; my only outward sign of panic.

He speaks to me like a father might to his daughter after she's misbehaved.

'You must think I'm an idiot . . . You should leave things that don't concern you alone . . . It's your own fault you've ended up in this situation.'

I found their marriage certificate. Dominic Reynolds and Morvoren Hicks. No death certificate, which unless it's kept elsewhere or we've committed adultery could mean Dominic and I aren't married.

I might have thought I was allowing my imagination to run away with itself, up here alone and with no one to talk to, growing increasingly paranoid with each hour that ticks by without a bite to eat or a sip of water to quench my thirst, had it not been for the wedding album I discovered beneath a pile of clothes that looked remarkably similar in fashion to those I'd found in the attic the other day. A blouse with a dark stain on the seam where the buttons had once sat, only one left dangling from a thin strip of cotton. In the photograph inside the velvet album there was one of Dominic and Morvoren's hands clasped together, the ring that's loose on mine fits snugly on her finger.

Buying your second wife the same ring as your first is creepy. But if that was the case, why is mine too big for me?

What clinched it however, was a sepia photograph of the lone bridesmaid carrying their rings on an ivory-coloured cushion, down the aisle. I felt a connective tug towards the girl whose hair and eye colour were identical to mine.

Then there's the fact that all the most important documents one needs to identify themselves have been hidden up here.

Until he shut me away in a locked room on the wing that I was unaware of, I had no idea Dominic had a screw loose, but is he sick enough to have duped me over my heritage?

DOMINIC

Then

It wasn't long after reporting Morvoren missing that I moved Kerensa into my bed and we began to live as man and wife.

But I digress.

The night terrors had hit my daughter almost immediately. The girl struggled to adapt to life without her mother and began acting out, and at the same time I started to realise why Morvoren had kept such a strict routine with her. It seemed that any kind of change led to caterwauling dramatics. I was struggling too, to keep on top of the housekeeping and childcare. I wasn't cut out for it. Thank God for the au pair.

I stared down at her CV. 'It says here that you used to be a teacher.'

'Teaching assistant.'

I'd never gone to school. My mother was always too drunk to remember to take me.

'What's the difference?'

'Well, a teacher teaches, a teaching assistant supports the child's learning.'

'My daughter doesn't go to school. Her mother is . . . not around and . . . there was an incident. She has . . . needs. I want someone who can help with her lessons.'

'You mean school her?'

'As well as mind her, and take care of the housework of course.'

'Well, I . . . I'm not sure I'm the best candidate really Mr–'

'No, perhaps not. I just . . .' I let the tears come then to emphasize my words. 'Since her mother . . . I never thought . . . I just don't know if I can do this on my own. It's a lot for one man to take on, you understand.'

I wiped my wet eyes and caught her sympathetic stare.

'Of course. I haven't had much luck myself recently.'

'No?'

'Well, I've applied for quite a few positions in the area and there isn't much demand for . . . what I do. I used to work for an affluent family a little further away from here and . . .'

'What happened?'

'What do you mean?'

'Why did you leave?'

'Oh, I see, right, yes, well, I . . . the man of the house, he . . . died. And the lady, she didn't cope very well. Took her own life. Slit her wrists in the bathtub. It was all rather sad.'

'So you're at a loss then, just as I am?'

'Well, I wouldn't put it quite like that but I suppose I don't have an income as such at the moment so I could do with the money–'

'Yes, the money. I'm offering above the typical rate.'

'I can see that.'

'Which I'm more than happy to increase to provide my daughter with someone who can home educate her also.'

'I see.'

I wrote a figure down on the woman's CV and pushed it across the dining table towards her.

Her eyes widened.

'The way I see it is you need a job and I need someone qualified to do it, so perhaps we could help each other out?'

KERENSA

Now

The kick comes as a surprise, though it shouldn't. Dominic's locked me in a room for however many days without food or water – long enough for my head to throb violently and the walls to seem to breathe – which means he's capable of anything. It knocks the wind from my sails, increasing the seasickness I get each time I try to stand on the floor that rocks below me.

'Ow!'

'You're not dead yet. But you will be soon if you keep refusing the food I bring to you.'

I sit and reach for the plate on the tray he's holding.

'I'll take my chances.'

He wasn't expecting it. The plate snapped in half easily. His own fault for using crockery instead of paper. It slices through his skin like a knife. The blood spurts across my chest and sprays his eyelids, rendering him temporarily blind.

DOMINIC

Then

I passed the doorway that led to the nursery. The au pair tracing a line of words with a manicured finger I could imagine wrapped round my cock, my daughter reciting each sentence with a perfect grasp of the English language. It was an image I wanted to capture. It reminded me of the times when my mother was lucid enough to sit down at the table in the small untidy kitchen with me to help me learn my sums. Before my dead-beat step-father made a re-entrance having spent half my five years in prison for various misdemeanours.

I don't know if it's because she caught my eye and wanted to get a reaction from me, acting out because she couldn't articulate the fact she missed her mother but she chose then to flip the book off the table, fling the jar of pencils at the au pair's face, and scrape her chair back so hard it fell against the floor with a loud *smack* causing two of the plinths to snap.

The tantrum lasted for most of the day. I had to carry her in the end – kicking and screaming, hair matted to her face with snot and tears – up the third flight of stairs and into her bedroom. Then sit leaning against the door, listening to her throw her toys and smash her furniture to pieces until her sobs receded.

She'd worn herself out by dinner time. The au pair made macaroni cheese and baked some packet mix bread for us to soak up the sauce with. We ate together at the dining table, like a family.

She stayed later than I was paying her to and waited until I'd put the kid to bed, meeting me outside, in the rear garden as she left.

I threw the chair on the bonfire, watching the flames shoot up then dance as they blackened the wood.

I heard her footsteps behind me, closed my eyes as I inhaled the scent of her sweet floral perfume. 'Perhaps it'll do you both some good if you were to spend a bit of time apart, Mr Reynolds.'

I frowned and she added, 'Sometimes when we're close to people we can't see what's right in front of us.'

'What the hell is that supposed to mean?'

'Your daughter, Mr Reynolds. She's . . . troubled.'

'Her mother's gone. Is it any wonder her behaviour is a bit problematic.'

'I think you've misunderstood me, Mr Reynolds.'

'I think I know exactly what you're insinuating and I don't like it.' I took a step closer, forcing her to back towards the fire. 'You're saying my relationship with my daughter is unhealthy.'

'No, that's not what I m–'

'You've got a filthy mind.'

'That's not what I was saying Mr–'

'Save it,' I spun around and stormed back towards the house.

I didn't mean to shove her onto the fire. But as I'd pushed past her she caught her foot between two of the rocks I'd used to contain the wood and stumbled arse-first onto it. Then her clothes caught alight. She might not have turned into a human fireball had she not been wearing hairspray.

I was in the corner shop the following day when I overheard two women gossiping about my late wife's disappearance, suggesting I must somehow be responsible.

'It's usually the husband isn't it.'

'And even if he didn't bury her somewhere on all that land something must have happened to her in that house.'

'Yeah,' the shop-keeper joined in, 'she's hardly left the place since she married *him*.'

'He looks the type, don't he?'

They took turns to agree with one another's assessment of me.

I took great satisfaction in my sudden appearance from the aisle at the furthest end of the shop. They obviously hadn't seen me enter behind the old couple who stank of lavender soap and cat piss.

'Mr Reynolds!'

'Nosy old bitches,' I nodded in greeting, dropping my full basket onto the floor with a loud smack and slamming the wooden framed glass door with the bell chiming behind me.

When I drove past later, on my way to dispose of the au pairs' cremated remains, I saw a huge crack running the length of the pane of glass and smiled to myself as I hummed along to the radio.

KERENSA

Now

He recovers quickly, stems the bleeding with his sleeve and towers over me.

I recall what Dr Linden said when Dominic commented on the stitches in my scalp. 'Wounds above the heart bleed faster and heavier and often look worse than they are.' The cut isn't deep but the floor is a bloodbath.

His features could cut steel, his penetrating eyes as sharp as the point of a blade. 'You're going to regret that.'

DOMINIC

Then

Gossip spread quickly in the village and everyone seemed to have plenty to say about me. I was the topic of conversation at dinner parties and the subject outside the school gates. It was nice to be thought of and I found it amusing to play up to their fears.

'Oh no, there's Mr Reynolds,' the boy with the ball said, as it rolled off the public field and onto the grass I was digging a hole in for no reason other than to scare the little shit who couldn't seem to keep away from the house.

'What's he doing?' his friend said.

'Dunno, but I'm getting out of here.'

'Leave the ball there. It's not worth it.'

My reputation didn't seem to put the au pairs off. But it didn't deter the police either.

I'd just stabbed the football with the tomato knife and stamped on the deflated leather I'd dumped in the pedal bin when the familiar car parked diagonally out front, its occupant knocking on the door a minute later.

I opened it to the man who was most obsessed with me, wearing a fake expression of surprise. 'Sergeant, what can I do for you today?'

I found the best way of dealing with them was to go along with whatever they asked me to do. You want to search the property, be my guest. You want to update me on the lack of leads you have about the ice-cold investigation into my wife's disappearance, please do. A teenage boy has accused me of stealing his football and threatening to throw him into the tin mine backing the house, where all the bones of the kids I've supposedly murdered are, no I don't mind you checking it out. The old biddy who runs the grocery shop at the end of the road alleges I broke the window in the door, yes officer the wind took it right out of my hand. The au pair who used to work for me has gone missing you say, no sir I hadn't heard.

There were others, of course, over the years, young and naïve but none as pretty as *her*.

And there were other stories too, some that were so vividly described they could fill a book. But the police couldn't determine the truth from fiction so there was never enough evidence to pursue a trial.

KERENSA

Now

I'm expecting a fist to come flying towards my face and duck, cowed, arms protecting my head, but he turns and walks away.

I stare at the door until my eyelids grow heavy, my limbs as weighty as anchors.

I won't sleep. I can't. He might come for me in the night – whenever that is – and smother me with a pillow, slash my throat or choke me.

Because I think I know now, what's going on, so he'll have to shut me up– permanently.

DOMINIC

Then

I was driving back from the supermarket, the suspension groaning in protest as I reached the curve of the hill leading towards the village, the engine exhaling it's last breath as I ascended the road that would take me home.

I steered it as far left as I could before it died.

'Oh, for fuck's sake. This is all I need.'

I had a tank of petrol I'd just re-filled and a boot packed with frozen food. With any luck it wouldn't have enough time to defrost before I managed to get it back to the house.

The problem with being shunned by the community and having chosen the money over keeping in touch with your wife's jealous friends was that when you broke down on the side of a country road, miles from home, you had nobody to call for help. I didn't have a licence either, and the car was still registered to my deceased wife. I'd got away with it so far because I'd renewed her insurance, there weren't any traffic cameras in the area, and the local bobby just assumed everyone who lived in these parts drove so they never bothered stopping and checking the vehicle as they routinely did in the U S of A if you failed to maintain it. There were no bald tyres or lights on it that didn't work, but it hadn't had an MOT in over two years and the last time I'd taken it to a garage was to have the air filter changed and my wife was still alive.

I should have put it in Kerensa's name.

But as luck would have it, just as the clouds gathered overhead and released a torrent of rainfall, a stranger stopped and offered me a ride.

'I'm sure glad you came when you did.'

'That's okay. I was just on my way home myself. Got a nice chicken to cook for dinner.'

'You far from here?'

'Bit out of the way. On the coastal road. The House at the end of the World we call it.'

'You got kids?'

'Two of the little brats,' she laughed, and catching my creased brow added, 'they're not mine. I'm a nanny.'

'If you're ever in need of a job I could do with one myself.'

'How old's yours?'

'Single fatherhood is hard,' I said, avoiding the question.

'Mine are almost grown now. It won't be long before I'm no longer needed. I'm covering for the lady who left them. She wanted kids of her own after she got married last summer.'

'So you haven't been with them long?'

'Eight months. But here,' she handed me a business card. Written on it was the name of the agency she worked for, along with their telephone number and website address. 'We're all vetted and CRB checked and the manager conducts random visits to see how we're getting on with the children.'

The last thing I wanted was some stranger turning up to the house unannounced.

'Thanks,' I gave my best impression of someone genuinely grateful.

'It looks like you've got company,' she said, signalling to Annika leaning against the side of the car parked in front of the fountain.

She pulled up alongside it and helped me unload the shopping but I stopped her from entering the house and carrying it into the kitchen.

'Really, there's no need.'

'Well, if you ever want to bring . . .' She was waiting for me to name my daughter but I wasn't about to incriminate myself so pretended to be busy fixing the carrier bags to my hands, their weight causing my fingers to turn purple and shake.

'I'd better get this lot in,' I spat through the pelting rain, turning a blind eye to Annika's narrow-eyed stare.

'If you and your daughter want to join us for a picnic,' she glanced up at the dismal grey sky, 'when the weather warms up a bit, we'd love you to join us.'

I didn't think the teenagers she was looking after would want a strange bloke and a kid half their age to spend the day with them and guessed it was more for her benefit than mine. She turned the card she'd given me over in my hand to display her number written in black biro on the other side and said, 'It gets lonely doesn't it, putting them first.'

'Yeah, it does.'

I felt her stare on my back as I stumbled up the steps with my wares and fumbled in my pocket for the keys.

She waited until I'd turned back to wave at her before she sped off.

I dropped my appreciative grin the moment I caught Annika's gaze.

'You told me to be here at 6 p.m.'

'I broke down, had to get a ride home.'

She snorted and held out her hand.

'Come round the back.'

'Why?'

'I don't like conducting business in public, it's common.'

I waited until we'd passed the kitchen window before I struck her. She fell to the ground with one punch to her temple. She dug her nails into the earth and tried to sit up so I kicked her in the face, enjoyed the snap of her jaw breaking. She groaned and whimpered as I dragged her by the ponytail she wore along the scrubby grass and along the bridal path towards the garage.

***

The sound of water dripping into the tin bucket was the first thing to greet me.

The second was the look in Kerensa's eyes as she pointed up to the ceiling and said unnecessarily, 'We have a leak.'

The third was the realisation that it was coming from the attic.

And lastly, that I'd have to go up there and investigate the source and, depending on the cause and how bad it was, get everything from the loft down the stairs and past Kerensa without her noticing before I contacted a roofer.

KERENSA

Now

I choke and splutter, drowning in water that tastes bitter and powdery.

A huge hand clamps over my mouth. A thumb and forefinger pinch my nose, forcing me to swallow.

This is how I die. Head tilted back against the chest of the man whose legs are wrapped round mine, arms trapped behind my back, forcing the water he's spiked down my throat.

He releases me as I begin to cough, pins me to the floor before I manage to stick my fingers down my throat to tickle my tonsils until I gag.

I sob without tears. I'm all dried out.

Limbs heavy, eyelids shuttering, I struggle against him as I fight for breath.

'I'm not your wife, am I?' I croak.

'Not legally.'

'Who am I?' I say, or think I do, as the world dims.

DOMINIC

Then

We ate our dinner late. Kerensa moved her food around her plate. She blurted out that she wanted to look at our wedding photos.

I tensed, reminded her we couldn't.

I'd told her they were ruined in the flood when the river overflowed during high-tide.

Why ask to see them now? Had she somehow guessed they didn't exist?

Women were curious, they liked to question things, analyse them. I should have known it wouldn't be long before she took after Morvoren. Her fate was destined.

The stench lasted six months. The smell was horrendous. I told Kerensa we had rats, that they'd died in their traps, their putrefying remains were the cause of the stain on the ceiling in the bathroom. I couldn't pay someone to fix the mess so I had to make do with YouTube and my limited knowledge of carpentry and plastering. I burned the ruined wood, along with the clothes Morvoren was wearing when she died, which I had to peel off her rotting corpse, because I knew – from one of the books in the downstairs library – that was how forensic experts identified people.

Morvoren had quite a collection of morbid tales. I hadn't had her down as the kind of woman to find violence and death appealing, but she continued to surprise me even after her own murder. I found a large dildo in her bedside drawer hidden beneath an decade-old copy of Playboy and, about a year after her burial, while clearing out her wardrobe, in a shoebox, an adoption certificate.

I stared at the wedding ring I'd torn off her leathery finger and spat on the woman who'd lied to me about my stepdaughter's biology.

They weren't linked by blood after all. The only thing they shared was a surname– mine.

KERENSA

Now

A wave of sleep washes over me, sucks me under, and I start to sink.

I don't know if I'm dreaming or hallucinating.

There is a tall, dark-haired, broad-shouldered man waiting for me on the other side of the ocean curtain.

'Dad?'

DOMINIC

Then

When we'd finished eating she washed the dishes while I put the television on. She delayed joining me by making my packed lunch for the following day and placing it inside a Tupperware box. I never ate her sandwiches. I preferred the pasty shop in the village. But I liked making her feel helpful, she had fuck-all else to do. I gave them to the homeless bloke who slept inside the tent in the doorway of the boarded up unit next door to the betting shop where I spent so much time she thought I worked there.

I watched a film while she sat beside me, fiddling with her wedding ring, eyes glazed. I stared down at her exposed knees, slid a hand up her dress and ran my knuckles along her thigh. She stiffened and pressed her legs together. Her eyes appearing to regain their focus in the same instant that my fingers reached the lace edging of her silk knickers. I leaned over her to peer down between her quickly heaving breasts and brought her hand to the zip of my trousers. While she pressed her palm against my chest, straightened her spine and gasped aloud, I reminisced about the skinny blonde with the flat chest and wide blue eyes I'd seen that morning.

When the credits rolled I retired to the bedroom, allowing Kerensa to iron my shirt and polish my shoes for the job she thought I had. I got restless if I didn't go out at least once a day and it didn't bode well for her.

By the time she reached the bedroom I'd thrown my trousers over the back of the ornamental chair and unbuttoned my shirt.

She hovered in the doorway, waiting for me to instruct her on what to do. She took her time to peel off her clothes, revealing the gooseflesh on her arms and legs, before lying on the bed, facing me. One arm beneath her head, raised on a pillow, the other casually draped in front of her breasts. Knees drawn up, one leg crossed in front of the other to display one creamy buttock. I flung the shirt over the arm of the seat and landed on the mattress beside her. Clamping one of her nipples between my thumb and index finger I squeezed it until she yelped.

The sound of her pain caused my cock to harden. I pushed my knee between her legs to part them and pressed two fingers into her pussy and finger-fucked her until my knuckles were wet. As she moaned and shuddered in climax I bit her neck and bunched her hair into a fist, which when tugged on emitted a shriek and caused her eyes to water.

I used to enjoy the challenge of overcoming her resistance, but the thrill was lost when she began to respond with pleasure, initiating it even, so I had to invent new ways to keep the flame between us lit, and I could only come when she was fighting me off her and begging me to stop.

I didn't know when I crossed the line or if I ever had one but there was a darkness in me that compelled me to hurt her that I had no control over, that I didn't want to restrain.

***

The pillow was damp and her hair stuck to her forehead, the sudden loss of body heat caused her to whimper. I peeled off the sheet and left the bed, looking forward to the soothing spray of cool water on my warm flesh.

We showered together, I liked watching the soap run down her breasts. I exited the bathroom ahead of her, entered the bedroom, and dropped my towel on the floor. A small white square caught my eye. I bent to retrieve the piece of paper and unfolded it to reveal a number. I recognised the writing from the shopping lists she made and instinctively scrunched the paper up into my clenched fist. My rage burned hotter with every step I took, so that by the time I reached the wardrobe I was murderous.

Annika hadn't just been to the house, but in it.

I dressed, then slipped the piece of paper into my trousers and headed downstairs.

I sat in the drawing room under the glow of moonlight and glanced down at the glass of amber liquid in my hand. I wasn't a big drinker, but the whisky was necessary.

I was sharing a bed with a traitor.

I emptied it then poured another. I wanted to dissociate myself from the image of choking the bitch.

KERENSA

Now

I read somewhere the dead can hear for several hours after their heart stops beating because the brain is still active. That is why care home staff talk to the residents when they place a blanket over them, tucking it beneath their chin and opening a window to dispel the scent of death.

Just because I can hear Dominic's footsteps recede that does not mean I'm alive.

DOMINIC

Then

I was willing to sit on the knowledge Kerensa had kept Annika's visit to herself had it not been for Annika's brother, who she'd not only failed to mention existed but who she'd not bothered to divulge she lived with. Now, thanks to his dramatic appearance, Kerensa would know I'd had a hand in his demise.

There was no one to hear her wail as I dragged her along the hallway and unlocked the door I told her led to the spare room. Our nearest neighbour was about a mile away.

'Get off me.'

She kicked out, scuffing the walls and scored lines down my flesh with her nails as I tugged her up the staircase and unlatched the door that led to the hidden wing.

'What the–'

There were windows in the largest room which was straight ahead but they were bricked up on the outside because of the priests hole which I never found when searching for it, assuming Morvoren had lied. Though it's possible it exists, no one had yet been able to find it.

The dust was so thick I could feel it clog my nostrils

as I pulled her down the dark and musty passage and into the room to our right, filled with storage boxes. The grime on the insides of the glass the colour of cloudy lemonade.

'Let me go!' she cried, right before I tossed her onto the filthy floor beside a bag of rubbish.

I trod on a pile of type-written lines on my way out the door.

She flew at me, slapping her palms against the wood as I slid the bolt across to contain her. 'You can't leave me here!'

'It won't be for long.'

After a couple of days without food, starved and desperate, like a caged bird, she'd eat anything I brought to her. And by the time she realised it had been laced with sedatives it would be too late for her to do anything about it.

Unconscious, she'd pen a suicide note with a little aid. Within it she'd take responsibility for knocking Annika out, driving to the edge of the river, strapping her into her car, releasing the handbrake and watching it sink.

Sergeant Ramirez was on his way out the door of the Las Vegas Metropolitan Police Department when Lieutenant Forest waved him over. He stood at just over six feet tall and weighed about an extra thirty pounds to Sgt Ramirez's 170.

'Sir?'

Lt Forest spun round without a word, and Ramirez followed him down the lobby and into the door on the right where the cold case reports were kept, the team reviewing them long since left for home, their hours far more sociable than his.

Forest headed for the cabinet below the window overlooking the main street, the low sun had turned the sky peach, streaking the room in flecks of gold. He pulled out the middle drawer and leafed through the labelled folders, withdrew one, and handed it to Ramirez.

'This is the only homicide case I haven't solved. Make sure you find the culprit before you leave.'

That wouldn't be for at least another twenty-three years, but the emphasis in Forest's words was on the fact he wasn't just retiring from the force having served his thirty-year stint, he was on a one-way ticket to the Man in the Sky.

If Forest was just leaving he'd have been able to investigate the murder of twenty-eight year old Imogen Leopold on a voluntary basis, but his recent medical had put paid to that. Pancreatic cancer. Six months the oncologist had given him. He was going to spend it on a sun lounger in Miami where the arid landscape would be replaced with an azure sky and white sand.

Ramirez opened the folder. On the front page, the victim's face stared back at him. Someone had digitalised the file, this was a photocopy of the original which was being held in the records department downtown, but nothing beat reading the witness statements and medical examiners notes on paper. Ramirez found he absorbed it better.

He turned the page and skimmed the list of persons of interest penned on a slight left angle. Imogen's boyfriend was questioned because he'd been with her that day, a neighbour had seen him leaving her apartment six hours before she'd been found strangled with the cord of her hair straighteners. Her estimated time of death had been in the window of time between the boyfriend driving home to get changed and then to the house of the woman he'd been cheating on his girlfriend with.

The DNA found beneath her fingernails matched the millionaire tycoon arrested for her murder. He'd been remanded in custody and bailed within twenty-four hours, and never taken to trial because he'd admitted to having had sex with her and one other woman in a drug-fuelled threesome in his penthouse. Everyone except one other man named 'Dom' had been interviewed. Though they had his DNA on the system it didn't match anyone on their database. Which wasn't surprising because according to the mogul's lawyer he was British. The trouble was, Americans were notoriously crap at differentiating British accents and when comparing the

Combined DNA Index System to the UKs National Criminal DNA Database there was no hit, which meant that unless the man was caught after having committed a crime here, there or elsewhere they might never find him.

PART TWO

DOMINIC

Now

I'm locking the door that leads up onto the wing when I hear the rumble of an engine and the squeal of brakes. I glance out of the bedroom window and down at the circular driveway to see the panda car parked horizontally in front of the entrance, seemingly boxing me in and preventing me from making a hasty departure. Not that I would: that would only make me appear guilty, and I don't yet know why they're here. Or could: my car is in the scrapyard.

I take my time to walk down the stairs and open the heavy oak front door to be greeted by a short, stocky constable and his tall, lanky male partner. Both men remind me of Laurel and Hardy. And both wear the same expression on their faces. Like they're expecting me to invite them in.

That's how the police are in Cornwall: countryfied, laid-back, trusting almost that even suspects are pleased to see them, to welcome them into their homes and offer them tea they are obliged to decline lest the man they've come to question has poisoned it.

But that wouldn't do. How would I explain the disappearance of two officers of the law as well as my wife, two au pairs, Annika's brother Franc, Kerensa, and the first piece of shit who took their last breath in my hands?

I widen the door and stand back, watching them enter, their beady eyes on me as I close it, and point to the lounge, the sunlight that streaks through the window pooling on the thin carpet. 'Please, take a seat.'

'Why don't you join us, Mr Reynolds?'

'I'll stay standing, thanks. How can I help you?'

'We have a few questions we'd like to ask you.'

I indicate for him to go on.

'We've received some information about a–'

'I'm guessing this is about Annika.'

He doesn't waste a beat. 'What's your relationship to Annika?'

'Miss Bergh's my housekeeper.'

'For how long have you employed her?'

'A few months. It's unlike her to leave me in the lurch, so I'm assuming something's happened to her.'

I pause as they look at each other expectantly.

'When was the last time you saw her?'

'A couple of days ago. She came to collect her wages.'

'Does she usually do that, turn up on a weekend to take payment?'

'No. Which is why it seemed odd.'

'So, why then,' the fat one says, 'have you not reported Miss Bergh missing?'

'If, as you say,' the skinny one added, 'she isn't the kind of woman to let you down.'

'You have a duty of care, you see, as her employer, to notify us,' continues fatso.

'Well someone did, otherwise you wouldn't be here.'

'Actually, we're here on another matter.'

And that's when I realise they're playing me. I'm

nought but a pawn in their game. That's what they do you see, they twist everything you say and turn it right back round on you, so you don't realise until you've already knotted yourself up, that they gave you the rope to hang yourself with.

I want to wipe the smirk I catch threatening to tug the corners of his mouth up at having caught me out but instead, as I know is expected, I sink onto the velvet couch opposite them and rub my dry eyes to redden the skin around them.

'My wife . . . just brings it home.'

'Your wife?' says the stick-insect, with a hint of confusion in his voice.

'Yes, four years she's been gone.'

The men exchange an awkward look this time, that takes them longer to break.

'I'm sorry to hear of your wife's passing.'

'Oh, no, she's not . . . She didn't die. She disappeared.'

The dull *thud* is loud enough to cause both detectives to turn their heads towards the ceiling.

The sedatives I gave Kerensa must have worn off.

They look back at me like cats staring at a mouse they've cornered.

KERENSA

Then

Ruby sang as she worked, a rendition of an old pop song Mum used to dance around the lounge to. The memory as sharp as a knife, cutting deeper when she started swinging her hips to the sound of the vacuum and kicking the air as she rocked her torso backwards and forwards, leaning into the hose before raising her arm and high-fiving me.

She reached down to switch the hoover off. 'Hey, I'm glad I caught you home. I need your opinion.'

She retrieved her phone from the pocket inside the sweater wrapped round her waist, began scrolling through it and handed it to me.

I stared down at the image on the screen. Ruby had taken a photograph of herself wearing a dress. I clicked back onto the album and hit the arrow button to view the next. 'What's it for?'

'A date. Saturday. He's a tad older than me but he's hung like a stallion.'

'You've shagged him already?'

'Of course,' she said, flinging her hair back.

'What heels are you wearing?'

'Black patent.'

I nodded and passed the phone back to her. 'The

blue one.'

She winked.

'What are you going to do with your hair?'

'Have it up.'

'Curl it and clip it. I'll do it for you if you like.'

I turned her towards the full-length mirror facing the wardrobe and lifted her hair off her face. Taking a strand of it and twisting it round my finger then letting it hang. 'You've got strong hair and it's in good condition. Ringlets will frame your features perfectly.'

She gazed at my reflected eyes and said, 'You look like her, you know?'

'Who?'

'You know who,' she said, nudging me with her elbow in a way that suggested a shared understanding I was oblivious to. 'His first wife.'

'Wife?'

'Yeah, Morvoren. It's a shame they never found her, isn't it.'

'What do you mean?' I stepped back reflexively.

'Oh!' she said, covering her mouth with her hand. Then leaning towards me and lowering her voice, added, 'You didn't know?'

'Know what?'

'She went missing.'

'Missing?'

I heard a creak on the stairs and turned towards the door.

'Does he never talk about her?'

Ruby's gaze followed mine as the door opened.

'What are you ladies whispering about?'

'Nothing,' I said, feeling my face flush.

'The kitchen's a mess.'

'I'll tidy it up,' Ruby said.

He studied her.

I crossed the room and stood at the window,

allowing the breeze filtering through the gap between the frame and the pane of glass to cool my skin as I listened to the sound of Dominic's footsteps recede.

I turned to Ruby, then to the vacant doorway behind her, tears stinging my eyes.

She crossed the room, took hold of my elbows, looked me in the eyes and said, 'You didn't know he was married, did you?'

'No.' I wiped my eyes with the back of my hand. 'Why didn't he tell me about her?'

She shrugged. 'You'll have to ask *him*, won't you.'

I could guess though, that he didn't want me to know because he had something to hide.

DOMINIC

Now

I turn a deaf ear to the distinct sound of Kerensa kicking something so that whatever it is rattles and clatters along the upstairs floor and into the wall directly above the lounge.

I should've given her a higher dose, or at least hogtied and gagged her in case she regained consciousness.

'Old pipes,' I shrug.

'Perhaps you could accompany us to the station?' Fatso says.

'It will allow us a bit more privacy and we could get one of our officers to sit in the playroom with your daughter.'

I disguise my confusion as I try to figure out why he would think Louisa was upstairs, realising quickly he doesn't know.

None of us can ignore the loud moan.

The Rake casts a glance towards the open doorway. 'Why don't you go and see if she's okay?'

'You never said why you came here.'

'We wanted to talk to you about the murder of Imogen Leopold,' he says, as another louder groan causes Fatso to reach for his radio.

KERENSA

Then

I contemplated how to broach the subject of Dominic's missing wife as I folded a towel and added it to the pile beside the rest of the laundry inside the basket. I hovered in the kitchen, wiping surfaces that already shone. He snatched his coffee as I stirred it. 'Are you trying to make a hole in the cup?'

He caught the fear in my gleaming eyes and brushed the backs of his fingers against my cheek. 'You look pretty when you're scared, like a fawn in headlights.'

I should have taken notice of the unease that raised the hairs on my arms but instead I focused on the fizzle of excitement that caused my nipples to pebble under his stare.

I swallowed my fear and said, 'Ruby told me about your wife.'

He glanced down at my cleavage and I saw the crotch of his jeans stir.

'She said that Mrs Reynolds disappear–'

He caught the rest of my sentence in his mouth.

I was too stunned to respond at first. Then too excited to think. It wasn't until he released me and stood back as I swayed, flashing his perfectly white teeth at me, that I recalled Ruby's warning.

Before she'd left, Ruby, stood at the door, and said, 'Just make sure you're not alone when you ask him about the late Mrs Reynolds, and don't be accusing.'

'The police think she's dead?'

'Mr Reynolds was their primary suspect for a while.' Then she frowned. 'Don't you keep up-to-date with the local news?'

Why are you working for a man you believe might be dangerous?

'I don't read the papers and we don't have internet.'

It didn't seem appropriate to continue questioning him with the scent of his aftershave on my skin.

DOMINIC

Now

There are far too many bodies on the property and I don't have enough time to dispose of them all before the cavalry realise Laurel and Hardy have vanished and come snooping, so after I've bashed the Rake's head in until his skull caves like his predecessors I lug him towards the basement and throw him down the stone cold steps. He lands on the cement with a crack beside Fatso.

I have to shut up the whining, snivelling whore upstairs before I can drag Franc's carcass into the basement with the dead detectives.

Pack first, you need to be able to make a quick getaway, comes her words from beyond the grave.

'Yes mother.'

KERENSA

Then

I tasted him on my tongue and fantasized about the way he'd pressed me up against the wall and, imagining him reaching up my skirt, yanking my knickers down, lifting me up and pushing himself into me, I pleasured myself in the bathroom. He must have crept up the stairs because I wasn't aware that he was eavesdropping until I opened the door, red-faced and he gave me a knowing look.

'What do you fancy for dinner?' I stuttered, in a high note.

'You,' he replied.

I tripped from the bathroom and stumbled down the stairs in my rush to avoid his blazing handsomeness.

He was business as usual when he returned home a few hours later. I spent the entire afternoon in a daydream, I couldn't get our kiss out of my head.

'He snogged your face off then gave you the cold shoulder?' Ruby said, as she dusted the lounge.

We discussed the *Cornwall Live* online news articles I read on her phone shortly before she left for her evening shift behind the bar at The Lost Goat.

'You didn't tell me about his daughter.'

'What's there to tell?'

'Where is she?'

'I assumed she lived here, with you.'

'Have you ever seen a girl in this house?'

'I guessed she was in school when I came to clean, considering the hours I'm here.'

'There's no evidence a child ever lived here.'

She squinted in confusion. 'You mean you didn't know about her until you read that article?'

'Something might have happened to her after her mother disappeared.'

'Perhaps that's why Dominic told me not to bother cleaning upstairs, maybe he wanted to preserve her bedroom.'

'There is no bedroom. No photos. No clothes. No toys. Nothing.'

Dominic had never done anything to make me feel unsafe, quite the opposite in fact.

I was standing in the porch, hadn't yet made it as far as the threshold and back into the tiled entrance after waving Ruby off when he arrived with a screech of tyres, bounded into the house, braceleted my wrist and brought me towards him.

'I've missed you.'

'You have?'

'I want you.'

'You do?'

'Yes,' he snarled into my ear, nipping my neck with his teeth then carrying me upstairs and kicking the door to the master bedroom open.

He threw me on the bed and ripped my clothes in his haste to get them off.

He liked me on all fours, facing away from him, when he thrust into me from behind.

'What am I going to wear?' I said afterwards, breathless, as I combed my hair straight.

He opened a cupboard filled with outfits and brought out a sleek button-down dress that hugged my curves perfectly and ended just above the knee.

'Where's your daughter?'

He shook his head and smiled. 'I've just fucked your cunt sore and that's all you can think about?'

I bristled at his choice of words.

'Next time I bend you over the bed I'll remember to stuff a pair of your knickers in your mouth.'

I was too shocked to reply which seemed to be his intention because he changed the topic by threading his fingers through my hair, weaving it up into a bunched fist, and searing the flesh below my earlobe with his hot breath.

'There are lots more things I'd like to do with you should you desire it but you must agree not to keep re-opening old wounds.'

I felt myself fall against him and sizzle like melted butter. 'Okay.'

'But, I can see how curious you are so I'll answer your question. Louisa is in boarding school.'

I opened my mouth to speak but he shushed me with a dark penetrating look that made me feel small.

'My wife was a depressive who drank too much. When she disappeared I became the prime target for scandal. My step-daughter developed behavioural issues as a consequence and in her best interests I sent her to a residential school. I don't like talking about the past because it prevents me from moving forward.'

My wife, he said, in the present tense, not ex. And *was*, as if he presumes that she is dead.

'I won't bring it up again.'

'Good. There are much better things I'd like to talk to you about. Like how sexy you look in that dress.'

I wanted to ask him who it had belonged to considering the label was for a shop that had gone out of business in the nineties, when I'd have been far too young to have worn it, but beneath the surface of our lust the air thrummed with danger. I didn't want to tip the balance.

'Maybe it's time to call it a day if your relationship or whatever it is that's going on between you is like standing on a knife-edge,' Ruby said, when I told her we'd slept together. 'And giving you his dead wife's dress to put on afterwards?'

'I don't know that it was.'

'You're right. It could have been his daughter's.'

'Urgh.'

'Exactly.'

I elbowed her.

'Seriously though, you should stop having sex with him, move out. He's technically still married.'

'Yeah, I know.'

'Didn't he instigate things with you when you began questioning him about his wife?'

'Who according to you is a ghost.'

'I bet she haunts that wing.'

'What wing?'

'You're telling me that you've never snuck around the house while he's out?'

'Of course I have. The only thing that's locked is the cupboard at the top of the stairs.'

'The first thing I'd have done when I found out who he was and what he's thought to have done is go snooping for that key.'

'Why haven't *you* then?'

'Who says I haven't.'

'If you had and you'd have found something you wouldn't have been able to keep your gob shut about it,' I laughed.

She retained her blank expression. 'I never told you what I studied in university.'

I folded my arms. 'Go on.'

'Journalism.'

I sighed.

'You want to know why I took the job here?'

I rolled my eyes. 'To spy on him.'

She shrugged. 'Keep your friends close.'

And your enemies closer.

'Why are you telling me this?'

'Cos you're just as curious as me. Plus, with you on-board, I can get the inside scope on Morvoren's whereabouts.'

'What makes you so sure I'll go along with it?'

'You will. You've already begun wondering who you share a bed with, haven't you.'

The pressure was on Ramirez to find out all he could about the high-class hooker's death before his boss hit the soil, and that meant re-evaluating every piece of evidence his colleagues had acquired during the original inquiry. It was the least he could do. Forest had taken him under his wing, taught him how good cops worked the beat, and when he'd taken the detectives exam he'd studied with him to ensure he passed. That was two years ago now, just five years into his career, and he was damned if he was going to let the old guy kick the dust before he could impart the news that the fucker who'd killed Imogen had been picked up and extradited to the U S of A.

He started by reading through the file Forest had given him, then re-interviewing everyone who Imogen had come into contact with the night she'd been killed.

Marty the Mogul was holidaying in Cancun, one of the prostitutes who'd slept with Dom that night had since died of a heart attack as a result of her cocaine addiction, and Imogen's boyfriend was serving thirty years for sexual exploitation and living off the earnings of the women he had working from the hotels, motels and inns, and whom he'd taken a percentage from in *exchange for their protection, which didn't seem to stop a punter from raping one of them. Which was why Ramirez stood at the door of the floor-level property where the boyfriend's mistress lived.*

He flashed the woman his badge.

'Just call me Callie,' she said, leading him into the sitting room, which was littered with toys and computer games, but smelled good, and she didn't look like she spent her social security on meth. Ramirez wondered what she found attractive about a guy who pimped women out to feed his expensive taste. He soon found out when she opened her mouth. Half her teeth were missing and those that were there were rotten to the root.

'I've been clean for fifteen months, got my kids back off my mum, still getting used to being the parent.' She scanned the chaotic room. 'Guess I'm still learnin'.

'How'd you afford all this stuff?'

'I retook my GED when I left rehab and got myself a job at Walmart after weaning myself off oxy. It don't pay much but it's more than I had spare when I was usin'.

'What was your drug of choice?'

'Anythin' that could stop me thinkin'. That's the reason people smoke crack and inject heroin.' She taps the side of her head, 'To stop us overthinking and overanalysing everything, which we're very good at.'

She'd moved around a bit since the incident but Ramirez was able to find her current address through the probation service. She'd been released from her last stint in jail for a shoplifting charge seven months ago, was now listed on the voting register.

'I'm re-working Imogen Leopold's murder. I've read your statement but I wondered if you could tell me about that night. With the passing of time you might remember something that didn't seem important during your interview but might be significant enough

to give me a breakthrough now.'

'It's been . . .'

'Four years.'

'You must be desperate.'

She must have seen the disappointment and frustration in his expression because she added, 'I couldn't tell you the day of the week back then.'

She went over her day anyway to appease him, from the moment she likely would have woke and where she thought she was living then, what she might have eaten, where she'd probably have gone to score, what time Imogen's boyfriend usually would've come over – after she'd collected the kids from school and delivered them to her sister's to babysit while she waited for her drug dealer to deliver her night-time fix.

'Pequeño Soldado was just someone who hooked me up when I couldn't pay for a script.'

'But you slept with him?'

'Not often. I couldn't always afford to feed my habit, but I didn't know him enough to be able to call him by anything other than his street name. I didn't find out his real name till his girlfriend's murder brought the cops to my door.'

Ramirez left wondering if Dom was just a punter and Imogen's death was connected instead to the drugs she was taking. The autopsy had concluded that she was a regular user of cocaine and had a blood-alcohol level three times over the state's drink drive limit. Just because she'd screwed Dom – if that was even his real name – it didn't mean he'd harmed her. But if she'd owed Pequeño Soldado, aka Floyd 'Shanks' Perry, money Ramirez was certain Imogen would have ended up with a bullet in the head instead of a cord wrapped around her neck, which was the kind of thing someone with less physical strength than will might use to end someone's life. And required an element of closeness to the victim that other methods of murder – such as a gun – did not. Which was how gangsters tended to execute people.

Either the person responsible for Imogen's death had nothing to do with the underworld narcotics trade or they were a drug user who was high at the time of the offence.

PART THREE

DOMINIC

Then

I was leaving the bathroom when I heard them plotting my downfall.

'You have to find that key,' Ruby said.

'And mooch around the rooms in search of what? You think he's got a body up there?' Kerensa said.

'You won't know unless you look.'

I feigned ignorance when I met Ruby at the foot of the staircase. I caught her eyes as she carried the dish towels into the kitchen.

'I'm heading out to get some milk. There's nothing worse than black coffee. Do you want a ride home?'

I knew she wouldn't be able to resist the opportunity. She obliged, hoping to do some digging while I took us to the derelict farm that had been advertised as having an on-site well, before the council discovered the land was built on a mine shaft and the owners were forced to take it off the market.

'M– my bungalow is t– that way.'

'I know,' I said without taking my eyes off the unlit road ahead.

She moved swiftly, like a cat, clawing and slashing with clear varnished nails as lethal as blades, which merely grazed my well-protected arms. When that didn't work to distract me she reached over and fought for the wheel, aiming for the guardrail ahead, hoping we'd crash, thus allowing her to scramble from the car, to escape. But I was able to maintain control and steer us onto the track leading towards the Frasier's old farm.

I stopped right beside the rusted gate that still stood between the posts that remained erect, two decades since the building had been condemned. She'd undone her seatbelt in preparation to jab me with the heel of her flat-soled sensible Clarkes. I punched her once, hard, in the side of the face so that her head bounced off the window, then again, cracking the glass and causing her ear to bleed.

Once I'd incapacitated her, I left the car and walked round to her side. She flopped into my arms and landed on the moss-covered path coated in evening dew. It was still early despite the coal-coloured sky and the tidal wind brought with it a wintery chill.

Her pulse was as fast as a marathon runners, her acting skills nothing at all like Morvoren's.

She waited until I'd stopped and raised her by the collar of her coat before scrabbling for purchase on the dry uneven earth. I held her over the deep dark pit that would become her tomb, her face bathed in the blue-tinted glow of the moon.

'W– why are you doing this?'

'You betrayed me.'

'Wait! Let me explain,' she tried a different tact.

'I won't let you get away with filling Kerensa's head with your ideas.'

'B– but I was right, wasn't I? You killed your wife. And now y– your . . .'

'Going to kill you,' I finished for her as I threw her head-first down the deep hole backing the stone ruins of the farm.

I drove home unable to recall the journey, too incensed to think of anything except the task that lay ahead of me.

Making a fool of me was unforgiveable, Kerensa too would pay for her deceit.

KERENSA

Then

I felt the wedge of money beneath the sole of my foot
with every step I took. I had enough cash to get a train
or coach out of town. Once I was far enough away from
Dominic I could call my sister, Cheyanne. It didn't
matter that we'd fallen out. Or that she lived in New
Zealand. I needed her, she'd be there for me. I had to
cut through the field though. There was too much risk
of Dominic spotting me if I trod the narrow country
roads to the bus stop. A taxi would take too long to get
here, and if Dominic saw it approach the lane leading
to the house, he'd know I was planning to leave. I read
somewhere once that volatile relationships pose the
most danger to women when they end them.

I was just about to grab my coat when he entered
the house looking dishevelled. A single bead of sweat
glided down his forehead. I dropped his wallet on the
parquet floor as he slammed the door and stomped the
grass off his shoes. He strode towards me. My veins
froze and I stepped back instinctively, catching my hip
on the side. I reached behind me for the phone, but
he'd already ripped the wire from the wall. I spun
round and ran for the stairs. Just as I reached the top
and rounded the corner he caught my ankle, forcing

me onto my front, arms trapped beneath my chest.

Every nightmare I'd ever had involved a man holding me down. It was my worst fear, and the one thing I refused to be a victim of. He could beat me, but he would kill me before I let him do what I was convinced he was intent on, once I'd managed to wriggle one hand below me to squeeze then twist his dick, allowing me to turn and see the determination present in his eyes.

'You're going to pay for that you sneaky little bitch.'

DOMINIC

Then

I felt my chest tighten in rage and cuffed her arm in my hand. 'I really liked you.'

She squealed and something fell with a clink from her hand. I collected the key from where it had fallen and a brief note of guilt glimmered in her eyes before landing on the lock on the door that led up to the third-floor staircase, and the rooms that had been blocked off from the rest of the house for two decades.

I dragged her along the landing. 'I should have known you were no different. You women can't help yourselves can you. You've got to interfere then moan at us when you don't like what you've discovered.'

'I don't know anything.'

We stopped at the top of the stairs. 'If that was true you wouldn't be afraid of me.'

'I won't tell anyone, I swear.'

I stared down the central staircase to the bottom step. 'It's too late. You're a liability.'

'Please, don't hurt me.'

I spun her around so she faced me.

'I won't say anything.'

'No, you won't. You'll never talk again.'

KERENSA

Then

I gripped the bannister. He was going to shove me down the stairs.

'If anything happens to me Ruby will know you had something to do with it.'

He smirked and shook his head.

'She thinks you killed your wife. She'll tell the police. It won't take them long to connect the dots between Morvoren's disappearance and my de–'

He flew at me so fast I barely had time to register his fist before it connected to the side of my head with an explosion of pain.

The last thing I saw before my skull ricocheted off the skirting board was his grin.

DOMINIC

Then

I hoisted her up and carried her over my shoulder. Blood dripped down my chest and she smacked her knee on the way out the front door. She filled the wheelbarrow, which I used to ride her down the private footpath that ran alongside the back of the house to the headland.

I breathed in the briny salt air and closed my eyes to my father, seated behind a shiny white table in the visiting room. The look of concentration on my mother's face reflected in the rear-view mirror as she drove us back from the prison. The gritty sand between my toes when we stopped midway home. The smell of gin on her breath as she leaned over me to tuck me in. The shadow that filled the gap beneath my bedroom door after she'd passed out. The way I crawled inside myself when he entered the room, my mind shutting down before he'd reached the bed. *He* being just one of many.

If my mother had been sober she would never have allowed those men into our home. If she hadn't drunk herself to sleep, they wouldn't have been able to do the things they'd done to me.

I lifted Kerensa up, careful not to leave marks under

her arms, which might lead the police to think someone threw her over the cliff.

She landed with a sickening thud instead of an unheard splash. Bent with my gloved fingers splayed across my thighs I glanced down to see her twitch.

It's okay. No one will find her while her heart's still beating.

***

The helicopter woke me. It's spotlight bold and bright against the navy star-speckled sky. The call disrupted my breakfast of grilled sausages, eggs, and beans.

'Hello?' I spluttered through a mouthful of coffee.

'Mr Reynolds?'

'Yes.'

'My name's Doctor Linden. I have a patient under my care by the name of Miss Jennings. You're listed as her next-of-kin.'

'I am?'

'The coastguard brought her into Derriford last night. She's in our intensive care unit. I'm afraid she's had an accident.'

He paused, giving me the option to add an 'Oh, dear' but I was already packing.

I'd have to leave the country before Interpol were informed and I became one of their most wanted.

'She's suffered some swelling and bruising to the brain. If she recovers it's likely, due to the fracture at the base of her skull, that there will be some long-term impact. There's also a small bleed in her spleen, which we're keeping an eye on. She's stable but the next twenty-four to forty-eight hours are critical. It's my duty to let you know that should you wish to see her, you'll have to make it your priority to do so. I can't say for how long she'll be in this state.'

Change of plan.

I have to get to the hospital, play the role of doting boyfriend, and pull the plug.

I reach Plymouth within the hour, skid through reception and past the nurses station where I'm directed by Dr Linden who tries to keep up with me, to the bed of the woman he suspects I love, which is why I don't correct him.

He must see the concern etched onto my face for he sits beside me and doesn't get offended when I shrug his hand off my arm.

'There is activity on the MRI, but there are a couple of notable patches where it is clear there is some resulting loss of signal connectivity: one being in the left cerebral hemisphere, which is responsible for controlling the functioning of muscles on the right, as well as thought, emotions, speech, and learning. And another in the cerebral cortex, which is relied upon for attention, perception, awareness and memory. We've placed her into an induced coma to allow her time to heal. And we've put a stent in her skull to measure the pressure. Once the swelling has gone down we'll reduce her medication. She'll be assessed by a neurologist once she's awake.'

'Can she breathe for herself?'

'Yes. The ventilation is a precaution due to the head injury she's sustained and the drugs she's on which as a consequence to pain relief and sedation lower the heartrate and blood pressure. Is there anything else you'd like to know?'

'Will she be able to talk?'

'We can't say whether or not there will be communication difficulties.'

'Sorry to interrupt, but I wondered if Mrs Jennings had any family we should notify?'

I turned and looked into the shit-coloured eyes of

the short woman who stank of cheap perfume standing a few feet behind me.

I didn't put her right about Kerensa's marital status but the mistake needled me, and it seemed like too good an opportunity to let pass.

'She had her phone in her pocket when we found her so we could look through her contacts, see if there's anyone we can call.'

'Her parents are no longer alive and her sister lives in New Zealand.'

'The brain's a clever thing,' Dr Linden said as the dumpy cow trotted off.

'It is?'

'Oh, yes. The neural pathways can reintegrate.' I must have looked confused because he went on. 'Imagine pulling taut a piece of elastic that's been cut. The part that's broken cannot be mended, and in time may wear further and fray, but the rest snaps back when you let go.'

'I don't follow.'

'We had a patient. I'll name him P. He had a stroke, came round unable to remember how to tie his shoelaces but spent the remainder of his stay on the ward speaking fluent Spanish. He'd forgotten the language since leaving secondary but could recall it as though he'd been born in Madrid because his neurons had altered their course.'

'You're saying she might not be left with any detrimental affects at all?'

'All I can say for certain is that we don't know.'

KERENSA

Then

My ears were ringing and my temples throbbed as I opened my eyes. Warm light filled the green room. A trolley crashed into something metallic. A voice I didn't recognise spoke.

'Kerensa?'

What a weird name.

'How do you feel?'

Weightless and dizzy.

A man entered the room. He wore a suit under his white coat. He had a friendly face.

'Hello Mrs Reynolds. It's good to see you with your eyes open.'

My eyes wandered down to my ringed finger. The diamond looked wrong on me and the gold band it sat on was far too big.

Dr Linden assessed my walking, talking, carrying, lifting, chewing and swallowing then suggested I continue practising to expand my memory which had frozen on the moment I woke up and met the eyes of the man who called me his wife.

'Will the amnesia be permanent?' Dominic asked him.

'The human brain is the most extraordinary body

part in existence. We only know what twenty percent of it does. Let's stay positive.'

I filled the gym bag Dominic had brought me with the items I didn't think were mine and aimed for the reception area where I was told to wait for him to collect me. But instead of sitting on a chair I continued through the automatic doors and into the noon sunlight. I had no money, had to use NHS provided crutches to walk, and because I couldn't remember where I'd been living before my accident I had no idea where to go.

I turned the corner towards the bus stop, maybe someone would take pity on me. There was no harm in asking for a couple of pounds.

I was seized from behind. 'Where are you going?'

I turned to face my captor. 'I didn't know where you were.'

I don't think he believed I'd gone looking for him but he smiled all the same. That false clown smile, like it had been painted on.

'Let's get you home, eh? I expect you're looking forward to a decent brew and something edible.'

I nodded.

The silence that filled the car was unnerving. The journey down the A30 interspersed with the aroma of manure filtering through the air vents.

I walked through the door of a stately home built on the peak of a hill, set into the cliffs, overlooking the Cornish Riviera.

I didn't belong.

I unpacked my gym bag, placed everything into the washing basket, and headed down to the kitchen where my so-called husband had made a pot of tea. I took two of the cheese and cucumber sandwiches that had been cut into triangles, put them on a plate and carried them over to the dining table where I sat and ate.

'Why did you pick me up?'

He narrowed his eyes.

I indicated my sticks. 'I'm just going to be a burden to you.'

He leaned over and took my chin in the palm of his hand and wiped the tears from my eyes. 'Nothing but death will part us.'

I spent hours in front of the full-length mirror staring at my slightly drooped right eye that didn't quite move at the same rate as the left. At my right arm that trembled constantly. And at the leg that didn't always cooperate.

I didn't recognise myself.

Every now and again I'd scour Dominic's features for evidence of his devotion, something visible to match those words. The only time he became passionate was between the sheets. And I didn't know what we enjoyed in that department.

I felt like an imposter.

DOMINIC

Then

I didn't want to be left caring for a cabbage but I couldn't risk her telling anyone I'd tried to take her life so I contacted the same civil law firm who'd dealt with the adoption – and got Kerensa to sign a form granting me power of attorney, so that I could advocate for her, and made an appointment with Dr Linden to speak with him on my own.

'The dysfunction to her central nervous system is most pronounced where her movement is concerned,' Dr Linden said. 'The memory loss though, appears not to be due to structural changes or disease.'

'What does that mean?'

'It's psychological.'

He gave me a leaflet titled: What is Dissociative Amnesia?

'I'm no psychiatrist but I'd say the recent death of her mother led to feelings of loss that were exasperated by the physical consequences of the accident.'

'That's if it was.'

Dr Linden looked at me as if I'd spoken aloud his own suspicion.

Her parents were dead. Her sister lived in New

Zealand at the time of her death. The last time she'd sent Cheyanne a text message from the phone the paramedic had bagged up, cleaned, and which I'd told Dr Linden I'd use to contact everyone on her phonebook was the morning of Ms Jennings' funeral. Shortly before I gave her the job of tending to the tasks men weren't equipped to do.

You can't be bothered to hop on a plane to help me clear out Dad's stuff? You haven't even called to see how I am since he died! I'm having grief counselling and taking anti-depressants. This being just six months since our mum passed away. I'm done with you.

If Cheyanne replied, Kerensa must have deleted it.

Kerensa couldn't remember her name, date of birth, address, that her parents were deceased, the row with her sister, or even that she had one, who I was or where I lived.

She was placid and pliable and trusting.

She couldn't walk far or fast.

She didn't know what she liked or disliked.

There were many pros to convincing her that we were wed. The only con being I'd have to put on my best performance yet.

KERENSA

Then

I awoke to a shrill scream. It sounded as though someone was being murdered.

I was bathed in sweat, the sheets stuck to my clammy skin like latex.

Dominic leaned over me, brushed the hair from my face. 'Shush, it's okay. You're safe here, with me. It's just a nightmare.'

'It felt so real,' I cried into his chest.

His touch soothed an ache I didn't know I had. He reminded me to take my medication, did the shopping, paid the bills, bought me cookery books from the charity shop in town, told me about our neighbours, where they lived, their names, their personalities and foibles, told me not to worry about money, that he had everything covered. I felt like a kept woman.

'How did we meet?' I asked him one day.

He hesitated then perched on the armrest. 'I was your employer.'

'What did I do?' I sat up straighter, cringing at the crick in my back.

'You were my au pair.'

'Like *Rebecca*.' I detected a minute tilt of his head. 'It's a book.'

'Ah.'

'I wish I could remember falling in love with you.'

It happened gradually, as I learned his ways and became used to them. But always, I was aware of this darkness that lurked within him. It lay beyond each look, each syllable, each action. Over time the fissures became visible, then more pronounced, and I wondered what it might lead him to do, and if, when he finally cracked, his molten rage would be directed at me.

The notification appeared on Ramirez's laptop when he was halfway through writing a report on the domestic murder-suicide he'd attended the night before, while cramming a chicken sub into his mouth. He retracted it instantly and slammed it down onto his crumb-laden desk as he read the message from CODIS.

He picked up the phone and dialled his first international call. Five minutes later, leaving his sub roll to go stale, he drove just below the speed limit to the other side of town, got caught in the rush-hour traffic, tapped the steering wheel harder and faster in impatience as he neared his destination.

The man's wife opened the door and smiled in recognition. 'He's not feelin' too good today.'

He'd guessed as much when he learned the man hadn't yet got to Florida.

'What I have to say might cheer him up.'

She led him through the house and into the room at the back where he found Forest seated in an armchair watching some gameshow on the television.

'Boss.'

'I'm not your boss anymore,' he drawled.

'You are today.'

Ramirez crossed the room.

Forest motioned for him to take a seat opposite. 'What you got for me?' he slurred.

In his younger years Forest had worked the drugs squad, pulling in gang members for shooting down rivals who'd dared breach their patch, and learning the routes the distributors took to run their product to the consumers on bikes. The irony was that Forest was now loaded on legal opiates.

'I've found our man.'

PART FOUR

DOMINIC

Now

I'm expecting her to be sitting on the floor with her knees pulled up to her face, instead her shadow is trembling behind the door. I fling it shut and her eyes go wide like a doe about to be slaughtered.

Not here, too messy.

Parking a normal car somewhere inconspicuous until you can respray it and swap the number plates with another isn't possible with a police vehicle. The interior would give it away. So I decide my best option is to use the advantage I've been given to get as far away from the house as I can before Laurel and Hardy's mates come looking for them. I know I don't have long. The in-built GPS tracker will alert the local filth one of their cars has gone AWOL once it leaves the county.

She's a fighter. I should've broken her ankles to stop her from digging her toes into the mud. I don't want her to dirty the car. The police have ways to figure out from where particular types of soil come from. I might be dyslexic but I'm not thick, despite what my mother used to say. I've read the title of the books Kerensa spent many afternoons curled on the couch under a blanket with. I even managed a paragraph or two before the jumbled words which continually reorganised themselves swam across the page one too many times and I lost my concentration altogether. The one titled: *CSI For Actors* was very useful.

She tries to wriggle from my grasp. But due to her healthy diet not only is she fitter than she once was but she's maintained a slim physique, which makes it easier for me to carry her out of the house to the car.

Kerensa rolls into the boot, wrists cable-tied so tight the plastic digs into her flesh, whimpering muffled with a scarf, her pleading eyes streaming with tears.

'Not long now.' Before you're dead and buried.

I slam the boot lid shut and scan the area before getting behind the wheel, turning the key in the ignition, and pumping the pedal hard.

The siren wails, blue lights cutting through the dusk as I chase my future through each red-lit junction we meet.

KERENSA

Now

I choke down a sob and force my breaths to regulate. My legs are cramped, elbows bound to my knees, wrists to my ankles, with cable ties as thick as watch straps.

He prepared for this.

He won't be heading for the main road into town. But he'll have to pass the American style diner built at the crossroads – the one Annika told me she'd bought a thick, creamy strawberry dream milkshake, burger, and fries in just last month – whichever route he chooses to take. Two and a half miles from the house. A five minute drive. 300 seconds. I count the time it takes for the bumpy road to even out, use my shoulder to raise myself as high as I can, for the tyres to slow, then cease rolling, Dominic to exit the car and lift the lid. My nerves rattling my bones.

DOMINIC

Now

The roadblock is six miles away on the A-road. The constabulary kindly warned me shortly before they realised I might have heard and the internal police radio cut out. The chopper is heading east, towards the B-road that leads through the countryside. I cut the lights on the lane, heading for the woods.

There are caves there, underground fortresses where even thermal imaging cameras can't reach.

The sound of her wailing – which reminds me of the sounds she makes when I pull her hair to force her head back and see her reaction as I thrust into her from behind – will go unheard.

KERENSA

Now

I've counted past 450 when the suspension begins to shake, the vehicle tilting left, forcing me back down. I shuffle up by my face this time, scoring it against the rough fabric lining the boot.

Where is he going?

I reach 550 and the car starts to ascend.

According to the map of the area I read in the library when wanting to research the place in the hope of remembering something of it, the only upward slant of land is the carne to the east or the forest, further south. Where the dense foliage covers a rabbit warren of caves, once used for smuggling and later, the mining of tin, according to a history textbook I read not so long ago.

The shafts were filled and bricked up and over with concrete in the shape of mushrooms and fenced off with first wood, then razor wire, then walls ten feet tall and roofs of aluminium sheeting doused in anti-vandal paint. But the cave entrances are covered only by grills. Animal rights activists were concerned about rabbits and squirrels slipping and falling through the iron bars and being unable to climb the distance back up through the gaps and getting stuck down there, so they made them slatted and removable. And added wooden steps to the interior of each. But they could do nothing about the lack of drainage as that would have meant sending workers down onto the two hundred year-old tram-lines that are filled with arsenic-laden rock.

If he decides to dispose of me there, no will ever find my body. But worse, if he leaves me in there alive, I'll starve to death with the sun as my witness, taunting me over my powerlessness. That's if it doesn't rain first, drowning me.

DOMINIC

Now

I'm too focused on the task of cutting through the gap in the trees, which swing back and hit the car as I climb the rocky terrain, to notice the flicker of lights on my tail. By the time I catch the distant hum of a car engine we're already out of sight. But the car is close. And if the chopper spots the heat radiating from the engine of the police vehicle I'm climbing out of they'll know it's recently been driven and that I'm nearby. We need to reach the other side of the woods before that happens. It'll be quicker if we walk. It's a risk. If they bring dogs they'll sniff us out, follow our route. But if we don't I'll get caught before we've reached the tunnel that leads directly to the bay, which according to my watch we have just under two hours to navigate before the incoming tide begins to fill it.

I switch off the engine and let the car roll the final few yards, the chopper cutting the air just a mile or so away now.

I get out and breathe in the damp air as I move around to the boot to raise the lid.

It's drizzling now, fine rain that feels like thousands of ice-tipped needles pricking my nose and hands.

She looks terrified as I flip the knife out of my

pocket to cut the cable-ties binding her ankles together, then the one that holds her wrists to her ankles.

I watch her struggle to sit, using her palms to bear her weight, order her to get out, and wave the flick-knife at her face. 'You try to run, I'll slash your throat where you stand. You try to scream, I'll cut your tongue out.'

She flips her legs over the side of the boot and jumps down onto the bracken with a *thud*.

I coax her ahead with a shove, then press the point of the blade between her shoulder blades. She yelps and stumbles forwards. It must have nicked her skin because as I withdraw it, it comes back with a tiny drop of fresh blood that glints green in the light from my watch and her coat has a clean rip in it.

It's not mine. I found it in the shoebox under the bed, along with the flick-knife, and a dozen other mementos of her husband's that Morvoren kept to remember her hero by, after his legs were blown off in the blast of a landmine that proved fatal when he caught MRSA in his Afghanistan army hospital bed.

Wet leaves slap me in the face as Kerensa plunders on, batting down the twigs and nettles for me. A bird shrieks in the tall trees, flaps, annoyed by us for disturbing its home. Kerensa slows and I jab her again, this time with meaning, and she hops right, allowing me to step beside her to see that we've drawn close enough to the caves that what lies in front of us appears to be a sheet of mist curtaining a black abyss.

'We're here.'

KERENSA

Now

I halt, mid-stride, and glance up at the cedar that smells of damp bark and where a nightingale calls out to its mate.

'Come on,' he hisses.

Behind the night-time chirping I detect something much further away that has a motor.

'Can you hear that?'

'Move!' he growls.

Hovering somewhere to the west is a helicopter.

I take another step onwards, in spite of the panic gnawing away at me from deep within. And as I do, from the corner of my eye I catch a flash, expecting a grumble of thunder to follow. A second later it appears again, remaining this time, causing Dominic to stall, and snatch a glance at the bright white beacon of light cast upon the tops of the branches. It's far enough away that there's a chance whoever they're looking for isn't him. But close enough that if they are they will.

While he's contemplating what to do I tilt my head slight enough he doesn't notice the minute movement, and using the ethereal spotlight upon the ground to figure out where I might run – heart hammering against my ribcage – I dart out of Dominic's reach, sprinting away from the sound the soles of his shoes make as they scrape against the sodden grit after me.

'Get back here.'

I zig-zag between the trees out of sight as fast as possible so that I can get as far enough away from him that I can slow my pace, move quieter through the brackish landscape towards the helicopter emblazoned with the words: POLICE, and find somewhere to hide out till dawn. But as my feet pound down the slope I slip, trip and skid on my arse.

I collect myself as something terrifyingly similar to an exhaled breath and loud enough to send my pulse racing closes in on me.

DOMINIC

Now

The whistle is human and reminds me of the kind someone might give to signal an instruction to a dog. The voice that follows is distinctly male, deep-throated, gruff, and echoes around me, bouncing off the surface of the rocks.

The hunter has become the hunted.

There is only one way to avoid detection and that is to lift the grill and climb down into the pit that's just a few metres to my right. But that means having to leave Kerensa, who knows too much, and who might find her way out of the woods and into the arms of a waiting copper.

I'm debating my best course of action when I spot movement in my peripheral, a branch swing wide and whip back into place.

I eye the cave, the soggy leaves, and take a deep breath.

KERENSA

Now

The dog is panting and slobbering and soppy and loving and for just a few moments I want to stroke him and let him lick my face in greeting, but I can't I have to keep moving. Dominic could be anywhere.

The whistle comes again, louder, closer. And then the figure of a woman, illuminated momentarily by the helicopter's searchlight is within my line of sight. I could call out to her. But then the dog startles, spotting movement behind me and barks a warning I take heed to, because my life depends on it.

DOMINIC

Now

Rain falls through the stone ceiling above my head and drips down onto my face. I zip my coat up to my neck and lower my chin to retain some heat as I turn my back on the miniscule light that glints against the iron bars from the searchlight and tread onwards, following the tight crevices of the underground cave system, once used by pirates, with my hands. That are frozen stiff, the tips of my fingers already numb.

I wonder how the roof is holding up in the rain, and instantly regret not making contingencies, packing a bag, withdrawing some cash. I knew this day would come, I should have planned for it better. That's a rookie mistake, one I can't afford to repeat.

I should never have let her live, picked her up from the hospital, brought her home. Kerensa was trouble from the get go. Observant, chatty. I should have made her fear me enough that even if she could escape she wouldn't want to, too afraid of what I'd do when I caught up to her if she did. I fucked up. And from that I must learn and move on.

I scrape my shoulder on a piece of flint jutting out like a spike and put my hand out to find the cave walls have closed in on me.

I've never been claustrophobic but there is something about being in the pitch black, underground, in such a confined space that makes each inhalation feel thick and short.

I continue on in spite of the sensation I'm heading into the unknown rather than the part of the cave system I was intending to follow.

A few minutes later, my foot slams down into a pool of water. I retract it, foot soaked, and dip my toe in again to test how deep it is. Not enough to worry.

I plough on, in spite of my reservations, follow the sharp curve in the limestone.

Too late, I realise this isn't the cave I investigated previously, when I stumble taking a step and my foot doesn't land. I grasp the walls either side of me to prevent a forward stumble however far down the drop goes but my hands slide almost completely off them so that I end up landing on my chest, winded.

I lie there for a few moments, trying to catch my breath, listening to the slushing symphony of water, rolling below.

The tide is coming in.

These caves can fill in minutes.

Many people have lost their lives miscalculating the sea's clock.

I have to turn around, go back the way I came, risk being spotted by infrared cameras, my heat signature giving away my location.

If Kerensa hadn't made a break for it, I wouldn't be here. I'm going to enjoy making her suffer when I get hold of her.

KERENSA

Now

I've been walking through the fog for what feels like hours, each mile weighing heavier than the last, my legs like jelly, when I see a break in the trees. A little further on I spot the outline of a car. But not the one we drove here in. This one has it's lights on, the engine running, and a man is seated behind the steering wheel, another pacing in front of it.

'Hey!' I wave both hands in the air to alert them of my whereabouts.

Both turn to face me.

'I need help!'

DOMINIC

Now

The sky glows white above the clearing, the sounds of the chopper having been replaced with the bass of music loud enough to draw the attention of someone seeking help.

I head for the group of youths, the engines of their souped up vehicles running in sync, the concrete below my feet vibrating from the pulsing music their stereos emit.

I leave the path and merge into the crowd of revellers, some swigging straight from bottles of spirits and dancing to the beat of the tune, others lounge round a campfire, sharing spliffs, talking shit under the belief that what they're saying is philosophical. A twenty-something-year-old is cooking chicken wings and ribs on a one-use BBQ, another is rolling around on the grass as high as a kite.

'Hi,' I say fixing on the Chef.

'Yo, you wanna bite, man?'

'Sure.'

He retrieves a chicken thigh, wraps it in tin foil, drops it on a paper plate and hands it to me.

'Cheers.'

'Which one's yours?'

'Mine's back that way,' I point in the vague direction I came from. 'Ex-police car.'

'No way.'

'Yes way. Bought it off a pal. Smooth ride too. Still got all the gadgets on the dash. You wanna come take a look?'

'Sure, bro.' He turns to a woman spinning in circles with her scarf. 'Kit, come watch the food?'

She ballets towards the aromatic smoke without a word.

I nibble on the chicken as we walk. It's hot, spicy, and after hours without sustenance tastes so good I can't be bothered to talk. I nod in all the right places as I listen to Dan discuss the 'weird shit he's seen in the sky', my interest only peaking when he asks me if I'm with the girl.

'Just appeared from the bushes about half an hour ago.'

'Yeah, we were ya know . . .'

'Ah, man. That's not cool.'

I stop, the police car in front of us, the partygoers revving the engines of their sportscars much further back.

'Why's that not cool?'

'Her teeth were chattering and she looked zoned out.'

'Zoned out?'

'Yeah, ya know, spaced. Too many cookies, huh?'

'Yeah, maybe.'

'Still, you shouldn't have left her.'

'Sorry?'

'Look,' he says, resting his hand on my shoulder like we're pals. 'You don't leave your missus when she's trippin'.'

It happens in seconds.

He taps my shoulder in a false show of compassion,

then turns towards the car, and says, 'That's a new model innit?' slowly turning back on his heels, eyes questioning.

But before he can utter another word I've unclipped the thick stainless steel keychain from his jeans and, as he tries and fails to rip it from my hands, I hook it up and over his head from behind, pulling it taut across his windpipe.

He splutters and jerks, until eventually falling limp and dropping to the floor, but not before someone approaching sees what I've done.

'What the hell?' he yells, then, running towards us, calls out over his shoulder for someone called Tristan to follow.

KERENSA

Now

The man stopped pacing, threw his cigarette butt on the ground, stamped it out and listened to my request to call the police in disbelief. He shared a look with his mate sitting in the driver's seat, nodded, then tapped the bonnet and told him to take me to the nearest police station.

'Here,' he says, removing his coat and handing it to me to drape over my shuddering torso, his eyes not leaving the narrow winding country road.

He turns the dial up on the heater and the stereo down.

The helicopter is long gone, the sky streaked only with sparkling stars.

'They just found the surfer.'

He catches the crease of confusion on my brow.

'That's what the helicopter was for. He rode the waves over to the cove on the other side of the cliffs. The tide came in and his buddy panicked, thought he'd been caught out, called the coastguard as a precaution. Good that's he's safe, eh?'

'Yes.'

'This dude, he hurt you?'

I blink back tears, but more come. He reaches into

the glovebox and pulls out a travel size packet of tissues.

'Thank you.'

'No problem.'

He parks up outside the pub, heaving with tourists who've spent all day on the beach sunning themselves into a tan and now want to booze it up till closing.

'You want me to wait for you? See you home?'

'No, it's okay. I'm not going back there.'

'Right.'

I exit the car. 'You might have just saved my life.'

'Take care of yourself.'

I step out into the road.

He gives me a salute.

I'm halfway across the road when I'm blinded by the headlights of an oncoming car. I'm expecting the squeal of brakes and the skid of tyres, not the driver to accelerate.

Dominic's face through the windscreen is the last that I see before the bumper smashes into my legs and I'm thrown in the air, landing with an agonising *thump* on the slick tarmac.

DOMINIC

Now

Her eyes flicker open and land on mine. There's not a hint of recognition behind her eyes.

Her face is swollen and bruised, eyes black and puffy, nose bloodied, her two front teeth missing, her legs cut and bandaged.

Her tongue sticks to the roof of her mouth as she lisps for 'Wa'er pleash.'

I hand her the plastic bottle, it pops as she removes it from her mouth, the liquid trickling down her chin.

'Fank you.'

I place it back onto the bedside table of the static caravan I broke us into last night. The holiday park closed for the winter. The caretaker ignorant of the fact someone on the run might use wire cutters to enter the empty park and take advantage of the facilities in the hope of staying out of the prying eyes of the police, who are combing the area for the missing woman and her fugitive captor.

It's been forty-eight hours since I scooped Kerensa up off the road, opened the rear passenger door of the car idling on the kerb-side, threw her on the back seat, leaned over the centre console to slit the driver's throat, kicked him out of the car and drove us across the border from Cornwall to Devon.

We passed rows of caravan parks, cottages and lodges before settling on Dean Haven Holiday Park. The palm trees, azure waterfront view, free amenities, and fully stocked cellar were just bonuses. What sold it was the fact the place had been closed down. The windows and doors boarded up with nailed-on metal sheeting that was easy to prise off with the crowbar I found in a shed locked hastily with a rusted padlock that hadn't been fitted correctly.

The place looked like it had been abandoned for the best part of a year. The tell-tale sign of unpaid bills shredded and left in the litter bins, a Monday in May circled on the out-of-date calendar hanging behind the desk in the entrance. A mouldy coffee cup glued to the shelf above the office chair.

The owners might come back one day, the building might be for sale, but for now it's the ideal place to lie low.

KERENSA

Now

I don't recognise the chipped plaster on the ceiling above me, the fusty smelling mattress beneath my pillow-less head, nor the endearing tones of my captor, who brushes the stiff bloodied hair off my aching jaw. But the way he smiles sweetly at me stirs something within that makes me want to hurl.

'I'm flying over to England to meet with the Senior Investigating Officer, see if there's anything I can do to aid the team,' Ramirez said.

'Take me with you,' Forest replied.

He looked at him, barely conscious, breathing like an asthmatic. 'Is that wise?'

'I won't be able to rest till that sonofabitch is locked up.'

He looked like he didn't have long to wait. If it was his dying wish, Ramirez was not going to let him down.

PART FIVE

DOMINIC

Before

Mum left her bedroom and waddled down the landing to the bathroom. She hadn't fully closed the door so not only could I hear her retching but I could also see the tears that stung her eyes as she ripped off a piece of toilet roll to wipe her mouth, and threw it into the toilet.

She left the bathroom shaking, a sheen a sweat coating her yellowed skin.

'Be a love and fetch me a can won't you?' she rasped, holding her extended stomach.

I did as I was told, not because I was afraid of her but because I couldn't stand the person she became when she hadn't had a drink. I needed her to swallow her medicinal can of Special Brew because without it she'd stutter and twitch until she collapsed, and had a seizure, often on the way to school, someone would call an ambulance and with nowhere else to go I'd have to call Uncle Pete. He wasn't a relation but without a family member to collect me the paramedics would have no choice but to call social services and, as my mother had warned me every time she came round, I'd be taken away and put in a children's home, where the kids lived in fear of cold showers, getting locked in dark spider-infested cupboards or beatings.

So I dutifully complied and even though it made me late for school I'd wait till the tremors had dissipated before suggesting we leave.

'Okay son.'

The adults stood in the playground, making the most of the time they got to swap gossip, sniggered and whispered as much as their offspring as we ran through the school gates. I'd missed registration again so mum started arguing with the teacher.

'You can't keep him in after school cos I've gotta get to work. I ain't got time to be waitin' around for him to sit in detention for half an hour.'

This was a once-weekly occurrence that always resulted in me leaving school thirty minutes later than everyone else and coming home to find my mum passed out on the sofa, some guy I didn't know leafing through her belongings or leaning over her comatose body with his hand down her bra, his other down his trousers. Sometimes they jumped up, shocked, and left. Other times they carried on, dismissing me, as though I was just an object, like a lamp.

I'd pretend I hadn't seen anything and head for my room, close the door, then barricade it with the wooden chair I'd nicked from a skip. The lock had been torn from the wood and dangled limply now, tinkling each time I closed the door. Ever since the man with the eyes of a tiger kicked it down and poured petrol over my bed as I lay beneath it on a puddle of urine, wishing he'd light the match he held out in his hand as he yelled at my mother to get down to the bank or into the bedroom.

'You're gonna pay me back one way or another so you'd better hurry up and decide whether it's with your giro or your pussy.'

'Okay,' she said, defeated, 'just keep the noise

down. I've got a lad ere, ya know.'

'Really, where?'

She must've pointed at the bed because he chose then to get on one knee to peep under it at me. As soon as he smelled me he pulled a face. 'Jesus woman, he's pissed himself.' He kicked the leg off the bed so hard it snapped in half, and fearing it might collapse, I bolted from below the bed and stood there in front of this strange man threatening to burn our house down in my yellow stained pyjamas.

'Go and clean yourself up you filthy little fucker.'

I was used to being called dirty and stinky, but never by grown men. And the worse they treated me the more I hated my mother for letting them.

KERENSA

After

I remember the crash. The pain. The sound of my
bones breaking. The way Dominic's eyes darkened
when he realised I was still alive, and the expression
that took over his face when he saw that I was
disabled. I'll never forget it. But with the man lying
dead on the verge of the road, the only witnesses to the
impact staggering blindly to my aid instead of dialling
999, the police station I was heading for having been
closed, not one uniformed copper present at the time
of the incident, and Dominic having burned the car
soaked in blood before jacking another from a
frightened woman on her way home from a night-shift
at the food factory before snapping her neck, no one
knows where we are. Which means my only way out
of here is to rest and recuperate, continue to feign
confusion and memory loss until I'm fit enough to fight
for my life.

DOMINIC

Before

I was stood in the gutter prodding a snail with a stick, watching its feelers retract from the intrusion when the woman across the street waved me over. 'Ere you go love,' she said, holding out a carrier bag as I crossed the road to pick it up. 'Just a few bits my boys have outgrown.'

'Thanks,' I said, tossing the stick onto the ground to take the bag from her hand.

'How's your mother?' she asked, every time.

I answered the same way each month. 'Getting better every day.'

'Them fits still 'appenin' are they?'

'Yeah.'

'Epilepsy is it? My friend down by the park 'as it. Nasty can be for a little 'un to see. You're a brave lad, ya know.' She knew better than to reach over and ruffle my hair. Last time she did I almost snapped her wrist, an automatic reaction any time anyone touched me, ever since . . .

'You know where I am if you ever need me. Day or night lad, alright?'

'Yes.'

'Well, you go on 'ome then and I'll see you next

month.' Then she winked and added, as I knew she would, 'There's a little extra somethin' wrapped up in a pair of socks for you at the bottom.'

She knew better than to tell me to keep it secret too. She was a dinner lady, and knew the school wouldn't take kindly to her ordering her neighbour's son to hide things from his mum.

'What you 'avin' for dinner?'

'Corned beef hash.'

'You eat it all. You look like you could do with fattenin' up.'

She meant well, but her words hurt all the same. I knew I was too thin, too pale, too weak to stand up for my mum when one of her boyfriends got handy with his fists. And it tore me up inside knowing I was helpless to prevent her coming to harm, which most often was when I wasn't around.

I was about to push the front door open when I heard glass smashing, a *bump*, and her latest beau's raised voice.

I leaned down to peep through the letterbox to check the hallway was clear, turned the key in the lock as quietly as I could, crept inside, then tip-toed up the stairs and into my room.

I dragged the wardrobe across the room, emptied the new set of clothes onto the pile of unwashed flea-infested fabric my mother had forgotten to wash, and pulled the chocolate bar from the folded pair Mrs Lathom had given me that smelled nice, and stuffed it into my mouth, taking my time to chew, savouring the taste.

I licked the thick caramel off the roof of my mouth and stuck my fingers in my ears as the thumping and screaming grew more insistent.

I knew what happened between a man and woman in bed. One of Mum's boyfriends had shown me a magazine once. It looked horrible and sounded violent, but there was something about it that made my crotch tingle.

KERENSA

After

They come in droves, five days after our arrival, just as I'm starting to think I'll lose the leg that's turned a mottled black and has begun to weep around the wound.

Dominic poured vodka over the open cut, sewed the flesh together with some cotton thread using a needle, and dressed it in gauze he found in the first aid cupboard, but my shin bone is still protruding through the wall of muscle. The analgesia he's been supplying me with no longer strong enough to contain the pain.

They arrive in stab vests. Twelve of them, I think, though I might be seeing double. They enter the building next door. Dominic left a while ago to fetch more food from the store at the other end of the holiday park. I pray they found him before they reached me.

I scramble up on my right leg, the knee on my left is facing west, and drag myself across the bed to the window where I begin frantically whacking it till someone hears.

Then one of the officers turns east and two others follow.

'No, come back!' I yell as loud as I can while

searching the room for something to smash the window with.

Dominic hasn't had to worry about me leaving. I can't walk. But now the police are here, there's no way I'm letting them leave without me.

One stops as if listening.

Has he heard me?

Then he turns away just as I begin to wave.

I grit my teeth and lean over the bed, dropping onto my hands and crawling across the floor.

Thank God I've been allowed to eat for the last few days. I can't imagine doing this on even less energy.

I've barely made it to the door when I hear, 'Police! Exit the building! Walk towards us with your hands up!'

Does that mean they've found him?

I scream, 'Help!' as loud as I can and haul myself up as close to the handle as I can without standing, but my hand is so damp with perspiration that it slips off and I land onto the shiny floor, jarring my spine. A nausea-inducing wave of agony burns down my leg and tears stream down my face.

I wipe my palm on my thigh and try to ignore how much water I'm retaining there.

'Come back!' I call, slamming my hand against the door as I wriggle the handle to free myself of this misery.

I hear someone murmur something illegible, then seconds later, 'Police, stand back!'

I shuffle out the way right before the door comes away from the frame, one hinge snapping, before it lands on the floor with a loud *smack*.

'Thank you,' I sigh.

An ambulance arrives ten minutes later. The man they were talking to as I tried to get their attention turns out to be a security guard who comes to check on the place with his Alsatian once a week.

'I noticed the lock on the food store was off,' he says. 'There was a bag of rubbish in the refuse bin. I thought maybe kids had got onto the property or a homeless person might be squatting, but with the recent slaying of those people up at that big old house . . . it was in the news that anyone noticing anything suspicious should report it, just in case the guy responsible was hiding out.'

'Well, I'm glad you did.'

'Me too.'

I'm air-lifted to a private hospital, somewhere south of St Austell. They operate. The sepsis has remained within the lower portion of my foot, so they might have to remove it. I tell them I don't care, I'm just glad to be alive.

I don't learn of the horrors the police encountered until the following day, when two of them enter the room and sit at my bedside to take my account of the events of the last few years of my life.

'You've found Dominic?'

The female detective with the short spiky haircut replies. 'Yes.'

Much later, I'm told he was discovered on the railway line, lying on the tracks.

The turbulence made Forest sick. Though that could've been the last of the chemo being expelled from his system, having given him an extra couple of months with his wife and older kids, which he'd chosen to spend in England with the guy who was no doubt going to nab his job when he croaked it. The journey was otherwise uneventful. It wasn't until they'd landed and Forest nicked the wheelchair the airport staff lent him because he was struggling to stay upright and walk at the same time that he realised he might be travelling home beside an empty seat, the lieutenant on another plane in a body bag. He played the apologetic phone call to Forest's wife in his head, interrupted by the cab driver telling them they'd arrived at their destination.

They spent a few hours in the lounge of Heathrow airport strung out on coffee, glazed doughnuts, and reading London guidebooks while they waited for the 9 a.m. flight to Newquay.

The hotel was about ten times smaller than any Ramirez had stayed in before, and the interior nothing like them. It was quaint, contained lots of wall art and ornamental comforts and, despite facing the sea, there was nothing inside the rooms to suggest it's whereabouts, which Ramirez liked. He hated those ocean-front properties with nautical-themed décor. As if you needed reminding all the time of where you were. Perhaps Forest could've done with something like that though, because he'd taken to wandering. It was a new affliction that was starting to grate on Ramirez.

'Hey, cut it out, you'll wear the shine off the wooden flooring.'

'Just testing my wheels on the decking.'

'Stolen wheels.'

'I'll bring it back when we return to Heathrow airport.'

Forest glided across the ground level floor one final time before stopping in the open patio doorway to light a Camel. He switched on the television using the remote control and inhaled a lungful of nicotine.

'What?' he said, catching the look of horror on Ramirez's face. 'It's not going to kill me.'

'No, but I might if you set the fire alarm off and get us kicked out of here before we've even slept off our jet lag.'

'Quit your damn moaning. You've got far more than me to be thankful for.'

'I'm going to leave you to enjoy this pity party on your own while I call Detective Inspector Enys.'

Ramirez entered the room he'd chosen for himself – as far away from the sound of gulls squawking as possible – and closed the door on the cigarette smoke behind him. He dialled through to the SIO, which in the US meant lead detective. He'd been studying UK legal terminology on Wikipedia the night before their 5 a.m. flight.

'DI Enys.'

'Sergeant Ramirez, ma'am.'

'Ah, at last we speak. How was your ride?'

'We had a bumpy start but a smooth landing.'

'Good to hear. Where are you?'

'The hotel that features in that British film–'

'The Witches.'

'You know it?'

'Every child who grew up in the nineties was terrified of it.'

'How soon can we meet?'

'I'd have thought you'd have wanted to get some rest, have a bite to eat . . .'

'We're far too wired, especially since we got your email.'

'I'll come to you. Meet me in the . . . lobby in half an hour.'

'I see you've been buffing up on your US terminology?'

'I watch a lot of American . . . shows.'

Sure, you do.

PART SIX

DOMINIC

After

I could smell the pork as soon as I spotted the glossy BMW through the bushes lining the road beyond the holiday park as I stumbled, blindly, over to the static caravan, arms weighted with tins, packets of food, and bottled water from the store. The pigs met the security guard at the gate, who was carrying a set of bolt cutters. I took my chance then to climb onto the roof of the portacabin that housed the reception, jump down over the wall and leg it.

I ran until my chest burned, over fields, through hedges and across gardens until I saw the railway.

How was I supposed to know the rail-line was out of service?

It was the British Transport Police who'd found me. After the assistant to the driver of the train that passed me by metres called and told them there was a body on the tracks.

I'd lain there for an hour and forty minutes, feeling the ice-cold metal track seep through the flesh at the backs of my legs, the sleeper pillowing my head causing my neck to ache. I closed my eyes and listened to the sound of the trees creaking in the wind, the sweep of heather on the heathland to my right, the crickets in the corn to my left, waiting for the inevitable vibration below my spine, the squeak of wheels, the smell of oil, the moment of pain, and the endless nothing thereafter.

Had I kept my eyes open I'd have seen that although the train was travelling in the right direction I was lying on the wrong line. And had I not shot up as soon as I realised, and ran down the tracks, disorientated by my survival, towards the station, the Network Rail worker sipping tea on a bench during his break wouldn't have dialled 999 to report the suicidal man holding up the next train to Penzance that was due to arrive at platform two in eleven minutes.

'You're lucky the signal switch was set to divert,' he said, escorting me towards the office to where two PCs stood.

'It doesn't feel that way.'

They recognised me immediately.

I swung round and ran around the side of the building and out onto the street, straight into the side of the waiting car, where another uniformed police officer sat.

I would've made it had his female colleague, carrying two sandwiches and two bottles of Sprite in one hand, leaving the café beside the waiting area, not had a taser in her other.

KERENSA

Before

Cheyanne was in the lounge swigging the coffee she'd made after her arrival. Her husband, Mark, an insurance broker, stood in front of the radiator, blocking the heat that swayed the curtains, his eyes on my dad's car on the driveway. A classic Ford. Cheyanne wanted to sell it to cover the cost of the funeral. I refused. The room had grown silent since.

'Car's here.'

I felt the blood in my veins cool.

I walked across the room, feeling as if I was wading through treacle, and opened the door as though something had possessed my body, in my mind my father was still alive.

I turned back, glanced over my shoulder at his armchair in the corner facing the television and imagined him sitting there watching snooker.

Cheyanne gave me a half-smile and placed a weak hand on my arm.

I shrugged her off and marched on towards the funeral car.

'Come on,' she said to Mark, steering him away.

He caught my eye as he passed me and nodded.

They both walked on ahead. The door to the funeral

car opened, and a suited gentleman with a tall hat gave me a solemn bow, and motioned for me to get in. He closed the door behind me and then off we went.

At the end of the street we turned right passing the entrance to the lake where Dad used to take me freshwater fishing when I was little. Me with my net, leaning over the shallowest verge, him much further with his rod.

The park where Mum used to take us girls after school for a picnic. We thought it was wonderful, but I expect now with hindsight, it was to save on washing up.

We cross the junction and turn left then past the bakery where our parents took us every Saturday after visiting our grandparents – both sets – for a bite to eat before heading home.

And the swimming baths where Cheyanne almost drowned. Surprising really, because although I had saved her when she began sinking and thrashing around by holding her waist up with my legs, doing the backstroke to get us to the safety bar, she spent her early twenties travelling the globe, diving in waterfalls, paddling along swamps, and white water rafting in turbulent rivers. The most exciting thing I'd done was accept a job offer from a stranger.

Well, the position of au pair was advertised, but I'd applied on a whim, desperate, since my father's passing meant I'd have to move out of the childhood home I'd returned to after my mother's death six months ago when I learned my boyfriend of two years had been fucking someone else. This, shortly after I'd maxed out my credit card to buy him a second-hand car which he'd used to drive to his mistresses house every weekend instead of working away as he'd implied. I was skint, penniless, broke. I had no option but to take it. Washing someone else's clothes, cleaning their toilet, and tidying up the detritus of their nights spent with women wasn't something I'd considered myself to be doing at the age of twenty-two. But the house . . . That grand gothic building over-looking the ocean, with its Victorian gardens and private lane, rooms filled with antiques and intricate ensconced plasterwork, beautifully designed tapestries, and the heady scent of spices in the kitchen that reminded me of the ones in the museums I'd visited on school trips. Those walls contained so much history: love, loss, and laughter. I wanted to know what it felt like to own such a gorgeous place. I was seduced by that house. And sometimes, when I'd finished my chores for the day, I would stand in a room, and pretend it was mine. That I'd commissioned the hand-carved furniture– made from stone or wood. That the man who stood in the doorway with his unsettling stare was watching me out of infatuation and lust. That I'd chosen the linen I folded and put away.

I found Dominic creepy. I couldn't comprehend how any woman would find his pushy, false charm attractive. He reminded me of those conmen who lured women out of their life's savings with fake promises of marriage. He was self-centred and only interested in discussing the worth of items, often asking me how much I thought something might fetch at auction. The following week that painting or piece of furniture would be missing and he'd be flashing his cash, counting it in front of me.

To make me jealous or intrigued? I was neither.

I considered finding work elsewhere, but he paid well, and I needed the money.

DOMINIC

After

The court smells of beeswax and pine. The seats remind me of the church pew I sat on at my mother's funeral. The public gallery is filled with the jobless who have nothing better to do with their day than to take a gander at the hopeless man in the dock.

The media have labelled me a master manipulator, a serial killer with no particular mode of operation, no preferred victim, no obvious motivation. This both excites and unnerves them. Hence why several journalists are seated opposite me, eyes on mine as they notate the silence on pads of paper because iPads aren't allowed inside the crown.

The bail hearing at the magistrates was a private affair. And most of those present for the trial aren't here to listen to my sentencing. The jury have returned to their jobs, children, and retirement without a second thought to me, to where I'll be sleeping tonight, tarred with the labels associated with femicide. The witnesses: a police officer, a psychologist, a crime scene investigator, a pathologist, have all played their role in the proceedings and are no longer required.

The only two who remain, sit in the place they claimed their own three weeks ago. I don't know who they are, have never heard them speak, but I suspect they are the detectives mentioned during the opening speech by the prosecution counsel. I expect Sergeant Ramirez is the Mexican one. And Lieutenant Forest is the one with the leathery skin, wearing the kind of shirt you see on westerns.

Kerensa braved facing me instead of giving her statement via Livelink. She spoke of her terrible existence in the house that felt like a prison, even before I locked her on the wing. Her initial fear upon discovering the birth and marriage certificate that I was her biological father, and that Louisa was the result of incest because I'd given her Cheyanne's date of birth. Her belief that I murdered everyone who grew close to learning what had happened to Morvoren because it would lead them to discover she wasn't the first person whose life I'd taken. The horror of finding out how many people had come close.

Annika's body had been dredged from the river, along with her brother's burnt out car. Franc's corpse and that of the two cops who'd been killed in the line of duty had been retrieved from the basement. Several skeletons were exhumed from the garden during the dig, after ground penetrating radar alerted the police to several 'areas of interest'. One of whom belonged to Ruby. Another, a teaching assistant at the local primary school who'd handed in her notice before taking a job as an au pair for a local bachelor and hadn't been seen since.

Had they searched the woods as thoroughly, they'd have found two others. The dog walker who'd allowed his mutt to shit on my lawn. And the drunk hippie with dreadlocks that looked like he hadn't used shampoo in a year and whose bonfire, in celebration of the solstice, had woke me up at 3 a.m. when the tree in the clearing where he'd chosen to camp out had caught alight.

Morvoren remained undisturbed.

Of course Detective Enys had spoken to Louisa, who knew nothing, protected by the insular world of St Augusta's Residential School For Girls. I'd thought it best after the tantrum that resulted in her slicing all her hair off with a pair of scissors before turning them on the au pair. I did my duty. It wasn't as if I couldn't afford it. Especially after her assessment by the child psychologist before her admittance. Oppositional Defiant Disorder and Conduct Disorder were her diagnoses, characterised by anger, aggression, rule-breaking, difficulties socialising, lying, and blaming others for her own misbehaviour. She receives the highest rate of disability benefits, entitling her to the best psychological care money can buy, and that's the reason my defence barrister struggled to dispute the theory I'd gained financially from her mother's disappearance.

Without Morvoren's body, the evidence I was responsible for her death was circumstantial at best, but that didn't matter because they had plenty of DNA to prove me liable for the murders of those I'd deposited within and around the property.

What sealed the conviction I think, was when the crown prosecutor brought up the similar way in which Mum's ex-boyfriend had gone missing, shortly after losing her long battle with liver cirrhosis.

He was the first to go further than the others, past unwanted hands groping and stroking, to the raw humiliating stab of pain no one should ever experience.

I was walking back from the crematorium in a daze when I saw him, older now, grey-haired, wrinkled, and slightly stooped. Though he still wore that you-can't-touch-me look in his eyes when he clocked me watching him from across the street. I left enough distance between us that no person nearby would suspect I was following him. Past the churchyard there's a lane backing a housing estate. He glanced over his shoulder as he came to stop at the gate leading to the rear entrance of a red-bricked terrace. He must have known there was no possibility he was going to see the inside of his council house again, because he continued on to the end, turning into the alley that backed the moors, which was where I did it.

I had no idea how much resentment and bitterness I was carrying until I'd exorcised it. I felt as light as a feather. But the nightmares of *him* were merely replaced by those of my being arrested for ridding the world of a paedophile, whom I knew was unlikely to have ceased his crimes after he'd grown bored of me. And so, after I'd bashed the nonce's head in with a rock until brain matter seeped from the fractures in his skull and decorated the moss, leaving him to the elements and wildlife of Bodmin Moor, my resentment built. Directed this time, at the woman who'd birthed me, promising to protect and nurture me, and who'd let me down.

I washed my hands in a huge puddle and headed straight for the nearest shop where I bought a scratch card. Winning that £40,000 allowed me to order a passport and book a plane ticket to Las Vegas in the hope of starting a new life there. But I soon realised that without qualifications, a green card, or a skill, I'd have to return to England and face the consequences of my actions. I was becoming increasingly desperate for a way out of a future marred by poverty and homelessness. And as my three-month excursion was coming to an end I was growing more frantic with worry. Until I chanced on that casino.

'What we need,' my solicitor said, 'is an explanation that will satisfy the judge. Get him on-side and you win over the jury.'

I ran a hand across my dewy forehead and sighed. 'What do you want to know?'

'All the bad shit that's been done to you.'

So I told him, everything. And my criminal barrister summarised it in her closing argument.

'His mother was an alcoholic.' She pointed to me and added, 'Dominic lost schooling because she often couldn't get up in time to take him. He had to steal food because she spent all her dole money on booze. She physically neglected him and failed to provide the emotional affection one expects from his mother. She also ignored vital clues that her son was being sexually abused by the men she brought into the one place Dominic should have had sanctuary, because they paid for her addiction. One of whom raped him when he was just ten years old. His mother sold sex to these men in exchange for the money to fund her alcoholism. And his stepfather, who spent more of his adult life behind prison gates than outside of them, regularly beat his mother in front of him.'

She advised me not to deny my crimes, said a guilty plea would see me serve my sentence in a better establishment if we played the mental health card.

'All rise,' the usher says.

Everyone zeros in on me.

'Dominic Reynolds,' the judge says to me, 'your violence towards the female sex is abhorrent. You claim to despise women, who you perceive are nought more than prostitutes because your mother was unable to prevent you from being mistreated by a couple of the men she dated, and whom fed and clothed you throughout your childhood due to her inability to hold down a job. Yet she is not here to defend her apparent inaction, thus your allegations cannot be supported. By contrast, the jury found your excuses a farce, declaring you guilty, and so I hereby sentence you to life in custody without the eligibility of parole for the murders of Sophie Dixon, Ruby Westlake, Franciszek Borkowski, Annika Bergh, Detective Constable Robert Holmes, Detective Sergeant Adam Rushford, Daniel Kettering, and Jeremy Hart. As well as the attempted murder, false imprisonment, and coercive control of Kerensa Jennings. Who you took advantage of by removing her of her identity and convincing her that she was your wife, for reasons unknown.'

KERENSA

Before

I shoved what I could into the cardboard boxes I'd found outside Iceland on my way back to the house after work. Having spent all day in the mansion on the cliff, returning to the mess left in the wake of my sister's rummage through our parents' belongings felt like a slap in the face. She'd taken everything except the photograph albums, leaving behind nothing of value. Cheyanne wanted to put the property up for sale as soon as possible, having brought her and her fiancés move to New Zealand forward since her corporate job offer the week before. I had no reason to contest it. I could use my half of the money to buy myself a flat.

I'd always felt responsible for holding things together, ever since I'd saved my sister from drowning, I'd made others' safety and happiness a priority. That's probably why, when several weeks had passed since I'd sat beside my father's coffin in the hearse, I'd broken down. The fact I was now an orphan hitting me as I polished the framed photograph of a uniformed soldier that was hooked to the wall above the dado rail in the wide entranceway.

'Who is he?' I'd asked, once upon a time.

'Louisa's biological father.'

I was surprised he let her keep it there in pride of place. Though it added a regal elegance to the space.

As if he could read my mind he said, 'The picture's cursed.'

'Really?'

'I've taken it down three times. The first time I hadn't even got it to the floor when all the lights cut out. Power cut. The first the area had experienced since the second world war apparently. It came on right after I'd realised there was nowhere to keep it and had put it back. The second time, I got it to the attic when a dead bat fell down the chimney and frightened Louisa so much her screams startled me and I dropped it on my foot. The third time, the doorbell went. I hadn't even managed to take it off the wall and went to answer it to find no one there. I gave up after that. I got the feeling he was meant to stay and that the only way he'd go would be with the building.'

'That's . . .'

'Spooky. I know.'

I didn't have him down as the kind of man who believed in superstition. But as I came to learn, there were two sides to Dominic, and most people only saw the one. It was only, I suppose, as I grew used to the way he spoke and behaved that I began to see little flashes of his other side. But by then it was too late.

The phone call to my sister altered the course of my life.

'The asking price is over-inflated as it is!'

'Why do you always screech when you're upset?'

'Cheyanne, I can't afford to uproot myself to another country. I don't have the luxury of another's salary to rely on.'

'It's not my fault our father left us with a tonne of debt.'

'I'm not saying it is, it's just that there are no affordable properties in the area.'

'Move somewhere else then.'

'I've lived here my entire life.'

'Exactly, it'll be good for you to get out of there, experience new things. What's wrong with renting somewhere?'

'Look, I could do with someone helping me. There's furniture I can't lift, piles of broken things Dad wouldn't let go of that need binning . . .'

'Hire a man and a van and a skip then.'

'Can't you–?'

'No, I can't.'

I ended the call, then immediately sent her a text.

'Would you like a glass of lemonade?' Dominic appeared.

'Please, thank you.'

I caught the expectant look in his eyes.

'I'm sorry, I shouldn't have answered the phone while I was working.'

'Don't apologise. I couldn't help overhearing though. You need a place to stay? Only, I have this huge house with more rooms than I have use for–'

'I couldn't possibly . . .'

'I insist. Rent-free of course, till you get on your feet.'

I should have taken heed of my mother's words in the back of my head.

If things appear too good to be true they most definitely are.

But after paying off the gas bill it seemed my father hadn't paid for five years, and prior to that had under-recorded the usage of for about ten, I was left with only half of my portion from the sale of my parents' house, which was, as Cheyanne had quite rightly stated, over-inflated.

He even offered to help me empty the property. 'I'm sure we could salvage some of the furniture if you want to keep it. Anything you don't want I can put the seats in the car down and take to the charity shop in town.'

He waited until I'd moved in and settled into a routine, spending my days working, and my evenings combing the grounds – on the beach in nice weather, or in the evenings settled in my room reading a book I'd nabbed from the library – before inviting me to join him for dinner.

He came across as a kind man, generous, if a little persuasive.

It was all a façade.

I was being played. I just didn't know it.

The sun breaks through two swollen clouds as Ramirez and Forest walk side-by-side down the steps, leading away from Truro Crown Court toward Enys who stands leaning against her car, waiting for them.

He folds Forest's borrowed wheelchair into the boot and then sits in the rear passenger seat beside him and stares out of the window as Enys pulls out of the parking space and indicates onto the road. The greenery is a shade brighter, the air not as dry as he is used to.

They pull up outside a pub that indoors smells of ale and roasted potatoes. Mouth watering, he shares a look of understanding with Forest, and ten minutes later they're both seated at the table with a mixed plate of meat and vegetables from the carvery.

Mid-way through a mouthful of turkey Enys asks, 'How's the investigation going?'

'The state have enough forensic evidence to convict. The witness has agreed to testify against Luke in exchange for a lesser sentence for accessory,' Forest says.

'No one gets a happy ending.'

Had it not been for the despicable actions of Imogen Leopold's murderer in Marty's penthouse once Dominic left the party, Dominic would never have been implicated and his crimes would have gone unpunished. Yet, had police not had a reason to interview him they'd never have known the identities of the two people who'd fled the party shortly after his departure, before Imogen's body had been discovered.

'I met Marty in the green room of a nightclub,' Dominic said. 'We got chatting and he invited me and a few others back to his for an after-party.'

'Who was present?'

'Me, Marty, Imogen, some dude and two other women.'

Dominic was able to disclose the names of everyone who'd partied in Marty's penthouse, which was how the LVMPD were able to identify the man whose DNA had been discovered on the cord used to cut off Imogen's airway.

He'd fled immediately afterwards. But unbeknownst to Luke, one of the high-end escort's showers wasn't working that morning so she'd sauntered into his en-suite, to use his.

'He was sleeping next to Imogen,' Zena told the interviewer.

'I heard them talking, then a woman yelp. It didn't sound like they were having sex. It sounded like she was being hurt.'

'What did you do?'

'I switched off the shower, threw on my dress, and burst out of the bathroom. Luke was straddling her. It looked like he had his hands round Imogen's throat. I panicked. He looked at me, his eyes were glazed. I ran. He chased me from the house. I managed to jump over a wall into someone's garden and hide behind their shed. Then this dog ran out of the back door and . . . he was slobbering all over me. I thought he was going to bite my arm off. Then this man, he told me to come in, let him

call the police. I was coming down off the drugs, I couldn't think clearly, I was paranoid, I thought he might harm me so I . . . I'm a coward.'

Thanks to Sergeant Ramirez's tenacity, despite being exonerated for Imogen's murder, Dominic's statement aided cops in finding two previously unlinked individuals (a man and woman). Luke was charged with her murder based on the testimony of the woman, and is now facing a murder charge.

EPILOGUE

It's been six months since I moved into my studio flat. Five since I began psychotherapy as part of my recovery plan. Four since I received the criminal injury compensation. Three since I applied to the state for supervised contact with Louisa. Two since social services approved the funds to assess and support our sessions. One since we first met.

I intend to do whatever I can to prove myself worthy of fostering Louisa.

That girl lost her mother then, confused and lonely was removed from school, isolated in a huge house all day and taught and fed and hugged by women who came and went so often she had no time to develop a bond with any of them. When she began acting out, as children do when they're sad or frustrated and they haven't been given the tools to articulate their feelings, her stepfather dumped her in a residential school where most of her peers had learning difficulties or additional needs. So that rather than asses her based on educational merit, while considering how her early years had contributed to her development, they pathologized everything she said and did.

Her care plan depicted a girl who on occasion

displayed a 'concerning lack of accountability' and a 'tendency to deny, blame others or become aggressive' when confronted over her dishonesty.

Of course she became defensive when challenged, she must have felt as though she'd been abandoned. First, by her biological mother who'd fallen pregnant underage – the records about Louisa's heritage were vague but I knew enough to ascertain her conception was the result of rape. Secondly, by Morvoren, who'd adopted Louisa shortly before the death of her husband – exactly one year to the day they'd begun fostering her due to a 'complete hysterectomy as a result of severe endometriosis resulting in early menopause and infertility' – and who then vanished five years later. And thirdly, by her stepfather, who failed to explain her mother's sudden disappearance to her, then sent her away from the only home she'd ever known when she began to show signs of not coping with the changes thrust upon her.

I will not let her down.

We have both known what it is like to be broken. We will each get the help we need to mend. And when she is ready, and we have the approval of the civil court, she will come to live with me.

Cheyanne would have told me not to bother involving myself in the girl's life, especially after all she'd been through. But she's not here. She was diagnosed with ovarian cancer within days of the argument I learned from the text message on the phone police found during their search of the house. I've since pieced together some parts of my past with Mark. He was able to tell me about the weeks after learning how advanced the cancer was, the initial operation to remove her womb, the tumours on her bowel and bladder, the first bout of chemotherapy, then being told the disease had spread to her stomach and liver.

'I wanted to call you, but Cheyanne insisted she would call you herself as soon as she was well enough. Only she never got better. Then when I did ring your phone it was no longer in use. I looked online and could find nothing since you'd posted on your social media accounts about having begun dating your boss. You weren't listed on the public electoral roll, and there was the funeral to arrange and I was grieving, and I guess I just got caught up in everything. I'm sorry. If I'd known you were in trouble I'd have got the first flight back to the UK and took that bastard's life for him.'

'It's okay,' I reassured him. 'You couldn't possibly have known.'

But it wasn't okay. He could have gone to the police and reported me missing, and when they weren't able to find me they would have been obliged to begin a murder inquiry. They might have found me sooner, prevented my head injury. But life is too short to harbour resentment.

'The solicitor found you by fluke.'

'Solicitor?'

'Shortly after your accident, he sent a text to your phone. Dominic replied. He sent a box containing Cheyanne's personal documents to you. Her driving licence etc. Thought it might help jog your memory.'

That explained how her birth certificate had got onto the wing.

'How old am I?'

'Twenty-six. Cheyanne was two years older than you.'

I'd regained the two years of my life I thought I'd lost. I was not going to waste it by focusing on the past.

I Don't Love You, the sequel, coming soon!

'Watch your daughter,' DI Enys said.

I should have listened.

But how was I supposed to know the danger I'd invited into our lives?

Or that Detective Inspector Enys hadn't meant I should keep an eye on those I allowed near Louisa, but the girl herself.

ACKNOWLEDGEMENTS

I'd like to say a huge thank you to my editors Jessica Knott, Leanne Braithwaite, and Heather Dubay. My proof-reader– Caz Bower. My cover designer– Jamie Curtis. My publicist– Liz Hearne. Social media marketing guru– Daniel Greenway. And blog tour organising wizard– Zoe O'Farrell.

And of course, my hero, Michael. Who, thankfully, is nothing like Dominic.

I must also mention here, everyone who has supported my route to publication and beyond: Kerry Watts, Caroline Vincent, Claire Harris, Sumaira Wilson, Gillian Godden, Donna McCarthy, Lucinda Berry, Claire Stibbe, Katherine Stansfield, Helen Phifer, Katy Johnson, Rose McClelland, Bev Jones, Sarah Simpson, Christine Stephenson, Alyson Read, Lynda Checkley, Dylan Jones, Andy Barret, Owen Mullen, Malcolm Hollingdrake, Robin Roughley, Richard Stone and Conrad Jones.

There are many more people who've travelled the journey with me. If I've missed anyone it's because there is not enough space to fit all your names here.

Louise Mullins writes full-time using the experience she gained in a prior life working in the field of forensic mental health, working with offenders and survivors of serious crimes.

To keep up to date with her latest releases, visit her website: www.louisemullinsauthor.com. You can also find her on Facebook, Twitter and Instagram as: @mullinsauthor.

Love crime fiction as much as we do?

Sign up to our associates program to be first in line to receive Advance Review Copies of our books, and to win stationary and signed, dedicated editions of our titles during our monthly competitions. Further details on our website: www.darkedgepress.co.uk

Follow @darkedgepress on Facebook, Twitter, and Instagram to stay updated on our latest releases.

Printed in Poland
by Amazon Fulfillment
Poland Sp. z o.o., Wrocław
12 August 2021

eae219af-5522-48ff-8a2b-c69a376f6ebbR01